FEB 21 2008*

SPRINGDALE PUBLIC LIBRARY
405 South Pleasant
Springdale, Arkansas 72764

SPECIAL MESSAGE TO READERS

This book is published under the auspices of

THE ULVERSCROFT FOUNDATION

(registered charity No. 264873 UK)

Established in 1972 to provide funds for research, diagnosis and treatment of eye diseases.
Examples of contributions made are: —

A Children's Assessment Unit at
Moorfield's Hospital, London.

•

Twin operating theatres at the
Western Ophthalmic Hospital, London.

•

A Chair of Ophthalmology at the
Royal Australian College of Ophthalmologists.

•

The Ulverscroft Children's Eye Unit at the
Great Ormond Street Hospital For Sick Children,
London.

You can help further the work of the Foundation by making a donation or leaving a legacy. Every contribution, no matter how small, is received with gratitude. Please write for details to:

THE ULVERSCROFT FOUNDATION,
The Green, Bradgate Road, Anstey,
Leicester LE7 7FU, England.
Telephone: (0116) 236 4325

In Australia write to:
THE ULVERSCROFT FOUNDATION,
c/o The Royal Australian and New Zealand
College of Ophthalmologists,
94-98, Chalmers Street, Surry Hills,
N.S.W. 2010, Australia

SHERLOCK HOLMES: THE GHOST OF BAKER STREET

Taking the advice of Orson Welles, Greg Hargreaves leaves America for London, so escaping the attentions of Senator Joseph McCarthy. A 'B' movie scriptwriter, he arrives with a brief-case, overnight bag and his typewriter. Soon he is looking for accommodation — and notices a familiar address in the classified adverts of a newspaper. Taking the rooms in Baker Street he becomes involved in murder and mystery as he discovers them to be haunted — by the ghost of Sherlock Holmes . . . ?

VAL ANDREWS

SHERLOCK HOLMES: THE GHOST OF BAKER STREET

Complete and Unabridged

LINFORD
Leicester

SPRINGDALE PUBLIC LIBRARY
405 South Pleasant
Springdale, Arkansas 72764

First published in Great Britain
by Breese Books
Cambridge

First Linford Edition
published 2008
by arrangement with
Breese Books
Cambridge

Copyright © 2006 by Baker Street Studios Ltd.
All rights reserved

British Library CIP Data

Andrews, Val
    Sherlock Holmes: the ghost of Baker Street.
    —Large print ed.—
    Linford mystery library
    1. Holmes, Sherlock (Fictitious character)
    —Fiction 2. Detective and mystery stories
    3. Large type books
    I. Title
    823.9'14 [F]

    ISBN 978–1–84782–110–2

Published by
F. A. Thorpe (Publishing)
Anstey, Leicestershire

Set by Words & Graphics Ltd.
Anstey, Leicestershire
Printed and bound in Great Britain by
T. J. International Ltd., Padstow, Cornwall

This book is printed on acid-free paper

The Ghost of Sherlock Holmes

Don't start, and pray don't leave your
    seats,
There's no cause for alarm;
Though I've arrived from warmer
    spheres
I mean you all no harm.
I am a ghost — a real ghost!
That nightly earthward roams;
In fact, I am the spectre of
Detective Sherlock Holmes!

Chorus

'Sherlock! Sherlock!' You can hear the
    people cry!
'That's the ghost of Sherlock Holmes!'
    as I go creeping by!
Sinners shake and tremble where'er
    this bogie roams,
And people shout,
    'He's found out — it's the Ghost of
                Sherlock Holmes!'

The man who plots a murder, when
He sees me flit ahead,
Forgets to murder anyone,
And 'suicides' instead.
An Anarchist, with lighted bomb
To cause explosive scenes,
Sees me, and drops the bomb, and
   blows
Himself to smithereens!

The burglar who's a-burgling, when
He finds that I'm at large,
Gets scared, and says, 'Policeman, will
You please take me in charge?
The lady who's shop-lifting tries
To put her thievings back,
And says, 'Oh Mr. Sherlock, I'm
A Kleptomaniac!

My life was more than misery;
Compelled to strut the earth,
And be a spy at beck and call
Of those who gave me birth.
But, now that I'm a spectre, all

Their misdeeds will recoil —
I'm going to haunt *Strand Magazine*,
Tit-Bits and Conan Doyle!

This popular Music Hall song was
written by Richard Morton circa 1894

1

You have the infamous Joe McCarthy to thank for any enjoyment you may get from this story, though I admit that I have never felt like thanking the Senator for anything. This is the point where I introduce myself, Greg Hargreaves, American citizen, born in Australia. I was taken to America at the age of eight and almost from that time I was determined to become a writer. In my dreams I would be a second Hemingway or Steinbeck, but in reality I progressed from a collegiate journal, through pulp fiction to writing scripts for 'B' movies. The tiny Litho Picture Corporation would buy the out-takes from a major thriller movie, show them to me and then get me to knock out some kind of a story that could use them all. Although it was an affront to my artistic temperament, I became a past master at not rocking the boat, making some sort of a living and hoping it would be a stepping stone to bigger and better things. Then early in the 1950s when I thought I had landed my first really big fish (to work an existing best-seller into a vehicle for Bogey) the mat was pulled from under me.

When I received an invitation to give evidence before a division of the Un-American Activities Committee, I was both amazed and terrified. Amazed because I was, and remain, completely disinterested in politics. My sin was evidently that I had written an anti-Hitler piece for a college magazine at a time now deemed 'too early to be just patriotic'. The big guy at the studio said, 'it's O.K. Greg, you just feed them a few names', but he made it clear that if I did not thus purge myself I would instantly lose my assignment and would not be able to work for any major studio. I think he suspected that I would be uncooperative and did not even await the outcome of events, giving my job to a writer who was guaranteed to make every heavy a Russian or 'a commie' at the very least. I crawled back to 'Litho', but even they would only give me hack work with no screen credit. I was doomed, and asked the advice of the only influential friend that I had.

Orson allowed me to buy him dinner and having demolished several entire roast ducks and a dozen jello desserts, he dropped a saccharine into his coffee.

'Got to watch my weight old man,' he said, 'I'm about as much of a communist as Onassis, but I have broken all their golden rules and would make a good candidate for one of the hearings. Indeed I have implored them to subpoena me but I figure they think if Hearst couldn't put me down, nobody can. I'm a forceful kind of a guy and I'd love to cross swords with them, but they just won't let me. Can you imagine the kind of a hornet's nest your uncle Orson might stir?'

He lit a huge corona and with his great big almond eyes completely untroubled by the smoke it produced, he gave me the benefit of his advice.

'You realise that it is all a storm in a teacup that will blow over within five years. It's hardly worth fighting. Indeed others have destroyed themselves attempting to do so.' The cigar had gone out because in talking to me he had not worked hard enough on it. He lit another match and puffed away, before adding, 'You, however, cannot afford to wait for this lunatic's fall from power, so you must go to Europe and with your American experience you could quickly make yourself a very large fish in a smaller pond.'

History would prove that Orson's advice to me was good and sound, even if it did present me with immediate difficulties. My lady companion, with whom I had dwelt for several years, was unwilling to either accompany me to Europe, or to hold the fort until the good times rolled. The result was a monumental row that probably will never be resolved. At least, I have not seen Cherry since that day.

In only days I was flying to London with just a briefcase, an overnight bag and a portable typewriter. My pockets were stuffed with outlines of ideas and a letter of introduction from Orson Welles. Since that time London has become so familiar to me that I find it strange to look back upon that first arrival. As I rode in the taxicab through the centre of the city, I recognised all the landmarks, for had they not featured in the scripts I had written so often? But the difference was that in fact St. Paul's Cathedral was not at the top of Regent Street, and Marble Arch was not the gateway to Buckingham Palace. (It had never mattered, because the folks in Davenport, Iowa and Piggott, Arkansas had known no better). However, the small private hotel on the Euston Road was authentic enough and I found myself at the age of thirty-three in a small rented room, with practically no luggage and just a few hundred dollars in my pocket book.

I took a stroll, at first just along the Euston Road and back again. Then I slowly began to explore the streets. I was both hungry and thirsty, so when I saw a bar with a chalked notice outside saying they also sold food, I went inside and looked around for a booth. There were none — just a long bar with a few stools.

Most of the patrons were standing, nursing huge glasses of dark-looking beer. There were no women and I could see that this was a place for serious drinkers. I sidled up to the bar and chose a curly looking sandwich filled with cheese and tomato. (When in doubt always order cheese . . . it can't go off . . . just get more cheesey like). I also asked for a short beer, quite unprepared for the verbal list of liquid delights; mild, bitter, mild and bitter, old and mild, light ale, dark ale, brown ale, stout, half and half — the list was endless. 'Just give me the best you've got' produced a huge glass, like an American quart, which, I was assured, was a '*Smacklins Engine Ten Penny* . . . I drink a lot of it myself'. It was quite the largest and strongest short beer that I had ever encountered. He handed me the sandwich on a plate and said, 'That's two and ten altogether, Guv.' I gave him three sheets of the stage money they had exchanged for my good dollars and was amazed to get two of them back plus a pocketful of silver and copper coinage. I was cheered by the thought that my small capital might last me longer than I had figured.

The guys in the bar seemed a jolly crowd with none of that reserve encountered in Englishmen visiting Los Angeles. A small man in a flat cap asked me if I wanted to 'see the piper?' I glanced around expecting to see someone about to play the flute, but when he held up a newspaper the 'penny dropped', to quote a British expression. As I took the paper I thanked him and something in my intonation made him enquire, 'Yank mate, are yer?' I admitted as much and he said 'Got any gum, chum?' which produced laughter all around. I worked off my bewilderment by buying them all a drink, which at those prices seemed like a good idea, but the jollity this produced was interrupted by the morose guy behind the bar shouting, 'Everybody out!' or words to that effect. We stood outside the establishment and, confused by the strong beer and the barman's sudden change of style, I turned to one of the flat capped guys and enquired, 'What did we do wrong. Why did he throw us out?' He

7

replied 'nuffin mate, it's closing time!'

Of course, I have since become familiar with the peculiarities of the British licensing laws but way back then I was left on my own, puzzled and clutching a copy of *The Evening News*. I found a small park style square where I sat on a bench and gave that journal the once over. When I had read the editorial, news items and theatre criticisms, I idly glanced through the pages of classified advertisements. The 'Furnished Apartments' were all giving addresses that were a mystery to me, save one. I came across an address that seemed to ring several bells in my mind at the same time. 'Baker Street, three furnished rooms and usual offices'. I scribbled the address into my notebook before discarding the paper. I had passed down and through Baker Street a couple of times during my explorations, but more than that the name seemed to stir something already in my mind from the past. All of this made me want to take a look at these rooms, to find out if I liked them and if I could afford them. Certainly I already liked the atmosphere of the street itself.

'Hudson House' was proclaimed in capital letters by the front door. A semi-circular fan of glass panels above which a classical bearded head peered down topped this entrance. The bell was an antique of a kind that I had never encountered before. One had to pull rather than push it. There were footfalls and the door was opened by a thick set, ruddy faced man of about sixty years of age, wearing a neat blue serge suit. He seemed quite well spoken, only occasionally lapsing into some sort of London dialect. 'You are in luck, sir, the rooms are still available, but they will soon be snapped up, mark my words!'

He took me to the top of a short flight of stairs to what he referred to as the first floor. (I still don't understand why the British number the floors in that way). The apartment which he showed me was pleasant enough with one large living room (as he called it) and two smaller rooms off it. There was a cupboard of a kitchen and a small bathroom with an antique water heater that he referred to as a 'geyser'. The furnishing were undistinguished but I could see that the whole thing would suit my present purpose.

It proved that I was dealing with the owner, a Mr. Hudson, who told me that he had inherited the building from his mother. She had catered to a single tenant for a number of years, for which she had been housekeeper as well as landlady. 'He was an eccentric gent who lived here all alone for years, except for when his friend, a medical gentleman, came to stay with him . . . sometimes for months on end. After the old bloke left to live on the coast, my mother lived here by herself until she died a few years back. Since then it has only been rented a few times on a short term basis.' There was something a little bit furtive in his manner, especially when it came to the matter of the rent. When I asked how much, he rubbed his chin and asked, 'Five pounds a week 'urt you?' He flinched slightly. I knew not why because even I, a visiting American, realised that five pounds a week was more than just reasonable. There had to be some snag. I asked, 'noisy neighbours?' He shook his head, 'No, sir. I live all alone on the top floor by myself, and the basement is only used for storage.' I tried again, 'Are there rats, mice or roaches?' He was indignant, 'Certainly there are no rats or mice, and as for 'roaches' I don't really know what you mean. Some sort of fish aren't they? We are hardly likely to have those.' I placated him with twenty pounds saying, 'Here is the first four weeks rent and if I like it we will discuss a long term arrangement.'

Mr. Hudson was delighted and as he took my four 'fivers' he handed me a key to the front door saying, 'Move in whenever you like.' That night I stayed in my hotel room but looked forward to moving on the morrow into my 'Baker Street rooms'. The phrase had a ring to it. It had style and class and, but I knew not why, it also had a nostalgic ring. I considered that my luck could have changed, for, thanks to the low rental, my small capital could support me for many months to come.

My first day at Baker Street promised

well. I unpacked my one formal suit and hung it in the closet of the smaller of the two bedrooms. (The mattress seemed better sprung than that in the master bedroom). Both spare shirts went into the dresser drawer. After spreading a few toilet things around the bathroom, I went out on a shopping foray, returning with milk, eggs, boxes of cereal and several bottles of beer. I looked around for the icebox but could not find it. I went up to the top of the building and tapped on Hudson's door. He looked very furtive indeed. He said, 'Oh, changed your mind already have you? Well you can't have your twenty quid back and that's a fact.' Astonished I said, 'Mr. Hudson, I'm quite happy with our deal. I only wanted to ask where the icebox is. I'm sure you showed me but I have forgotten.' He reddened and said, 'Oh, please excuse my outburst, sir, I have had some private domestic problems lately. Icebox? I suppose you mean some sort of fridge . . . there is nothing like that. You don't get new-fangled gadgets for a 'fiver' a week.'

I soon realised that without an icebox I

would have a deal of spoiled purchases on my hands, so I made a mental note to stick to canned goods in the future. I made myself an omelette with some of the milk and eggs and was sitting eating the last of it when it happened. As I pushed the plate away and reached for my coffee, I sensed a presence behind me near the window. Once or twice as I had been eating I had fancied some sort of unexplainable reflection in a picture frame but had thought it a trick of the light. I had experienced strange feelings before, of course, as for example when wandering in the wilderness alone. If there was something in the room that should not be, I did not really wish to see it. I had been assured that there were no rats or mice, but Hudson's furtive manner earlier told me to steel myself for what I was about to see.

At long last I turned my head to look towards the window and wished then with all my heart that I had not. Darwinians claim that there is some primeval reason for that raising of the small hairs at the back of the neck. I can't accurately explain why this happens but I can testify to its occurrence. I gazed through partly closed eyes at a figure standing, framed in the window, whose presence I could not account for. Even through hooded lids and against the light I could see that it was the figure of a tall, elderly man, spare of frame but erect of stance. As he made no threatening move, I opened my eyes more fully to take in the details of his appearance. He appeared to be about seventy five with a high forehead. He was not transparent or anything like that, but something about his almost colourless face and unbelievably gaunt features suggested to me that he was a ghost, spirit or shadow . . . I know not what to call that in which I had never seriously believed! He wore a faded crimson dressing robe over a white shirt and dark morning trousers, while at his scrawny neck was a paisley patterned bandana. His feet were encased in neat leather slippers and on his head he wore a deerstalker. He raised a thin, clawlike hand in a gesture which was elegant in its style. The picture he presented told me at once just why I had been able to rent these very presentable rooms for next to nothing. They were unrentable to anyone with a head screwed on better than mine. Indeed the building was probably unsaleable for it was haunted, and here stood the resident ghost in person. A great many thoughts ran through my mind in those first seconds of this realisation. Some of them I can no longer recollect, but I do remember that after the initial shock I felt no real fear. After all, I had done the apparition no harm so why should he wish me ill?

At last it spoke, fixing me with gimlet eyes, quietly, but with a very incisive tone. 'Really my dear fellow, I wish you would try and behave in a less erratic manner. I find it quite irritating the way you rattle your cutlery.' I had recovered my nerve enough to reply warmly, 'Forgive me, but in sensing your presence I banged my spoon upon my coffee cup to scare that which I thought might be a rat, mouse or simply a figment of my imagination. You are the first ghost that I have ever encountered.' He smiled tolerantly and

15

replied, 'I do not much care for that definition to be applied to myself. I am not living, that is certainly true, although it took me quite a long time to realise it and reconcile myself to it, upon my demise back in 1930. I had lost my 'Boswell', my only friend, Doctor John Watson, earlier that same year, and had passed the three score and ten years suggested as a life span by biblical prophets. I had been sound enough in health and spirit for the whole thing to be an unwelcome surprise. It was most inconvenient too, for I had begun an experiment with my bees, which could have proved to be of scientific interest.' He smiled, kindly enough now, his parchment skin stretching over his prominent cheekbones in an eerie manner.

Quite suddenly, in my mind, the penny dropped. His reference to a Doctor Watson concentrated my mind on thoughts that should have arrived there earlier. Watson, Hudson House, Baker Street . . . in fact 'rooms in Baker Street'. I gasped, 'You are Sherlock Holmes!'

The old guy in the red dressing robe

held up his hand in what Sir Arthur Conan Doyle would have described as an admonishing gesture. He said, 'My dear fellow, I was wondering how long it would take you to reach that deduction. After all, I am certain that Doyle's writings based upon Watson's scribblings have found publication even on the west coast of America?' I asked, 'Is my dialect that distinctive?' He said, 'Yes indeed, my dear chap, tainted as it is with a hint of the Australian outback.'

I had been raised on Sherlock Holmes, my father having had a collection of back issues of *The Strand*. He and I would go up to the attic, lie face down on the floor and read them aloud together. That is to say we would each play designated roles. I always had to play Moriarty, Mrs. Hudson or Lestrade, never getting my ambition to play Holmes! I was emboldened to enquire, 'Is the good Doctor not here also?' (I felt that even a ghostly Watson could bring a ray of sanity to this bizarre situation). Sadly he said, 'Alas no, though I am happy for my dear old friend that his God-fearing style of living and

17

strength of character earned him a place in paradise. As one who has always questioned everything, including the possibility of an afterlife, I naturally could not be allowed to join him in what is popularly referred to as heaven. As it is, I must forever frequent those places that I knew in life. I spend quite a lot of my time here, but from time to time I take myself off to Fowlhaven in Sussex, where I spent my retirement. I also entertain myself by visiting Simpson's in the Strand, the Royal Albert Hall, the British Museum, and I often walk in Regent's Park and visit the zoological gardens. Even this robe that I am condemned ever to wear seems to elicit little surprise in these places where eccentrics are so often to be seen.

One thing still puzzled me, and as it was a delicate matter I brought it up rather hesitantly, 'Mr. Holmes, forgive me, but I had always understood yourself, and the good doctor, to be figments of Sir Arthur Conan Doyle's imagination. Obviously I am wrong in my thought that a fictional character cannot have a ghost!'

18

Holmes looked at me aghast, and again he raised that pale clawed member in the now familiar admonishing gesture. He all but hissed, 'You used that word before, please don't. As for your suggestion that Watson and I never existed, you can ask Hudson about that if you like, for his mother was my housekeeper. Poor Hudson. I sometimes feel guilty about reducing the value of his property, but what else can I do? I can't live at Fowlhaven all the time, and anyway, I prefer it here. Speculative builders have spoilt the Sussex coast.'

Sitting in the living room of what must surely once have been 221B Baker Street, (or that which had passed for it), actually conversing with Sherlock Holmes was a situation that I had never predicted for myself. I tried to regain my good manners by saying, 'Mr. Holmes, would you care to sit down and take coffee with me?' Suddenly he was no longer standing by the window and was sitting in the chair opposite to me across the table. There had been no intermediate stage. One second he was by the window and the next in the chair. He said, 'Thank you. I am able to sit, stand, walk and lie down, and all with the added ability of missing out the various tiresome stages of transition. I cannot eat or drink though. In fact, nourishment is not required which I count as an advantage. However, I cannot move existing objects or even turn the pages of a book. In order to read I have to peer over the shoulders of others, which is considered as extremely ill mannered by some. Another major disadvantage to my present situation is in my inability to enjoy tobacco or certain other stimulants at first hand. I suppose you have no strong tobacco? A foolish question, for I observe from the stains on your fingers that you smoke cigarettes quite heavily. Perhaps forty a day?'

As I produced a pack of Chesterfields I introduced myself, 'Greg Hargreaves.' I shook out a cigarette and lit it with my Zippo, noting Holmes' seeming pleasure at the resulting smoke. 'Thank you, Mr. Hargreaves, and perhaps tomorrow morning you could purchase some strong shag . . . 'Scottish Mixture', for example?

You will find the old clay pipe laying around in one of the drawers if Hudson has not been monkeying around. Oh, yes, and I would be obliged if you could make this room a little less orderly. In life I did not enjoy regimentation and still prefer disarray. I feel sure that we will get along splendidly my dear fellow.' He said this as I obediently started to strew my few personal effects around the room, with even the contents of my briefcase in some disorder. He grinned and asked, 'Do you think you could light another cigarette?'

Then we sat by the fireplace, for although the season did not require much heat it seemed a focal point. Holmes pointed to the coal scuttle and said, 'You will find it a good place to keep cigars.' It was my turn to grin, 'I must look for a Turkish slipper in which to keep the 'Scottish Mixture'.' He nodded kindly. 'You really are an aficionado! The nail is still there from which to hang it.'

After perhaps an hour of pleasant conversation, I suppose I must have nodded off. I awoke to find Holmes studying my effects and strewn papers.

He smiled as he turned towards me, 'Ah! My dear Watson . . . that is, Hargreaves . . . you needed that nap did you not? Come, you have been through quite an ordeal lately. Had you remained in the United States you would have been required to give evidence before this Un-American Activities Committee this very day I notice.' He pointed to the subpoena that lay upon the table. He asked, 'Will you be so kind as to turn the page that I may read further.' I did so, and having studied the leaf which followed he said, 'You have no charges to answer. I know the American Constitution well enough and my knowledge of American law is extensive. You may hold any political opinion you wish, or belong to any political organisation if you desire, and express your opinions openly, short of incitement to anarchy. Do they imagine that you are a communist?' I replied, 'No, I don't think they do, but they cannot find enough real communists to justify their existence. I, and others like me, are scapegoats.'

Holmes said, 'This McCarthy is a

dangerous fellow who poses as a patriot to advance himself. Beware the flag waver, for patriotism is the last stronghold of a scoundrel. Why did you not stay and call his bluff?' I told him about Orson's advice. He said, 'I have read something of the pompous Mr. Welles. Was it not he who said of me, 'A man who never lived, but will never die?' Well, I both lived and died, so ignore his advice in the future.'

Sherlock, or rather his apparition, had been busy among my effects whilst I slept. Busy enough, in fact, to have learned quite a lot about me. 'That you are American by nationality and Australian by birth we have established. That you are a free agent, I have deduced from your style of dress, both worn and in the wardrobe in the second bedroom. You are a writer I can see. I thought as much before I saw your papers through a study of your hands.' I knew all about those tell-tale indentations which frequent use of typewriter keys produces on the fingers. I asked, 'How, then, did you know that I was not simply one who operated a typewriter for business purposes?' He laughed, 'A businessman would employ typewriter operators, or, even if he did not, the indentations on his fingers would be evenly distributed. Only a writer would type with just two fingers and two thumbs and get away with it!'

It was my turn to laugh as I did indeed have an eccentric method of operating my portable Remington, hitting the keys with the two index fingers and the space bar with the thumbs. 'Anything else?' I asked. He said, 'Well you did not tell me when you arrived in Britain, but I can tell that you have been here hours, rather than days.' 'How?' (I was fascinated). 'Well, your packet of Chesterfields still bears the California sales tax label. You smoke heavily enough to have already started on the duty free cigarettes that I feel sure you would have purchased at the aeroplane port had you been here longer. Oh, yes, and I perceive that you have had a long lasting association with a red-haired woman.'

After a few moments thought I said, 'Well, I appreciate that you have seen the photograph in the silver frame, signed 'To

Greg, All my Love, Cherry'. In the absence of any sort of tryst ring, or mark made by one on my fingers, I also understand how you would assume a long standing relationship rather than a marriage. But Mr. Holmes, how the heck can you tell from a black and white picture that she has red hair?' He smiled indulgently, 'Elementary, Hargreaves, I hardly think that she was christened Cherry on account of having a red nose!'

No longer being alive had done nothing to reduce Holmes' powers of observation and deduction. When I finally turned in that night it was not until I had seen Holmes glide into the master bedroom, assuring me that he was able to lie down and rest, even if denied the luxury of sleep. 'I don't miss it, Hargreaves, I always begrudged wasting a quarter of my life in slumber, but I suggest that you get a good night's sleep. You look as if you need it. I shall simply rest and contemplate.'

2

'Everything O.K., Mr. Hargreaves?'

It was early on the following morning that the enquiry came from Hudson as I passed him on the stairs. I looked back over my shoulder as I reached the front door and said, 'Oh, yes, thank you. The rooms are most comfortable.' He looked relieved and asked, 'Nothing unusual then?' I replied mischievously, 'Well, now that you mention it, I have experienced something strange in the atmosphere, rather like the aroma of strong tobacco clinging to everything.' As his face fell I hastily continued, 'But don't worry about it, because I am a heavy smoker and I don't find it objectionable.' Thus I kept him on his toes for the possibility of an even further rent reduction, but did not overplay my hand lest he would do something drastic that might spoil every-thing, such as redecorating the place or putting in contemporary furnishings.

I tried three stores before I located the 'Scottish Mixture' that Holmes had asked me to procure. Eventually I tracked it down to a little old shop that had an imitation Scotsman outside. He was in a skin with a beehive on his head, evidently in the act of taking snuff. He was the British equivalent of the American cigar store 'Wooden Indian'. The old guy who served me looked like an antique too. He said, ' 'Scottish Mixture' . . . we don't often get asked for that now, sir, but I think I can find some, somewhere. Why yes, here it is, in the bottom drawer. Many years ago, when I used to help my Dad in here during the school holidays, there was a medical gentleman who used to come in for it quite regularly. Always said it was for his friend who must, I think, have smoked a great deal of it. Watkins I think his name was . . . or was it Watson?' I asked a daring question, 'You don't think his friend was the famous pipe smoking detective?' Then he really threw me, 'Sexton Blake? Not a chance. He was just a made up character in the boys' books.'

My next port of call was a shoe store

where I was surprised to find I could purchase a pair of Turkish slippers. I had to buy the pair because they would not sell me a single slipper. I had to pay extra to have a loop fitted to the right hand slipper that it might hang from the famous nail. They looked at me strangely in the store until I told them that the slipper was for a friend who had lost his left foot. The 'smart alec' clerk asked if I could not save money by advertising for a guy who had lost his right pedal extremity!

Holmes was delighted with my purchases and supervised the hanging of the slipper and its filling with tobacco. 'That's right, Hargreaves. Loosely . . . don't pack it tight. If you have the clay you might make a start with your pipe smoking career.' I had glanced in all the drawers and had indeed located an elderly clay pipe as well as a calabash and a straight briar. I crossed to the sideboard, opened the appropriate drawer and took out the clay. As I did so I noticed a bulge under the lining paper and my curiosity made me raise the blue paper to reveal a cabinet sized picture frame. I brought it forth and turned it over to discover that it contained a very old sepia photograph of a beautiful woman, dressed and coiffured in the style of the eighteen-eighties. Holmes raised both of his claw like hands in a gesture that suggested both surprise and delight. 'You will find it is inscribed Irene Adler!' He had no need to say more for as a Sherlock Holmes buff from way back I was able to say, 'It is the portrait of 'the woman'.' The one that any man would die for and all but caused a *Scandal in Bohemia*. He directed my placing of the picture in its frame on the mantelpiece, that he might easily be able to see it whenever he wished. I remember musing that Miss Adler was possibly leading some angelic choir, using her earthly operatic talents. Had Holmes been a more God-fearing man they could have been together in paradise.

Most of that afternoon I sat puffing at the clay pipe and filling the room with tobacco fumes. Holmes was delighted, and when I flagged a little he said, 'You don't have to inhale my dear fellow, just blow the smoke in my direction.' His advice was good, for my lungs were not used to such strong doses of nicotine, though in the ensuing weeks they became used to it, as did my palate. I was able to give the room a Sherlockian atmosphere without discomfort to myself. I did what I could for Sherlock Holmes from respect and through intense interest in the situation in which I found myself. For the first week I stayed close to the house and spent many hours in conversation with the sage of Baker Street. I had a million questions for him concerning his work, published, known, and even more fascinating, his undocumented exploits.

My stake, the wad of bills in my pocket book, was getting thinner though not yet dangerously so. But I knew the time had come to get to work. I discussed this with Holmes who was surprisingly helpful with an unusually shrewd realisation concerning my craft. He said, 'I have been to the cinema a number of times in recent years. After all Hargreaves, I don't have to pay to get in. All I need do is appear in the theatre at a time when there are plenty of empty seats, at a *matinée* for example, and sit there without challenge or question. I even saw a cinematographic version of one of my most famous cases, *The Hound of the Baskervilles*, in which I was represented by an actor called Basil Rathbone. A handsome fellow in a lean sort of way. I was quite flattered (he chuckled) but I'll wager poor old Watson would have been furious at his portrayal as a stout pompous idiot! He was far from that, Hargreaves. Watson was of average build and nearly as tall as I. As for his mental capacity, his intellect was far in advance of the average and all that separated us in that respect was his innocence and trust in others. That and the fact that he had not spent many years of single-minded study in criminology. Also he was not ruthless in his nature. I would have pursued my own grandmother had she been guilty of a crime.'

I puffed his clay and responded, 'Mr. Holmes, there were instances when you showed great leniency toward wrongdoers, for example, the Barrymores when they aided the criminal Selden, so I think you do yourself an injustice regarding your humanity.' He nodded reluctantly,

'Perhaps I exaggerate to make my point. Well Hargreaves, I realise that you have a living to earn, so please feel free to follow your own activities when you must. I am grateful to you for co-operating with me as you have, for you have no idea how irritating it is to be confronted with persons who scream hysterically when they realise that one is no longer in the land of the living. It does not happen too often for I have learned to blend with others in public places. But some of the people who have rented these rooms from Hudson became almost frightening in their terrified reactions. Usually I would take myself off to Fowlhaven until they had moved on, which usually was not long, but you see my house in Fowlhaven has been altered out of all recognition. I am never too happy there for long. I do, however, appreciate that you have a living to earn. Do you have any prospects in view?'

I told him of a letter of introduction that I had to people of importance in the British film industry. Orson, I told him, had given me such a helpful opportunity for a meeting with the producer, Lyle

Garrison. He knew nothing of Garrison, but to my surprise he knew a little more than I had expected concerning Orson. 'Ah yes, our pompous friend, Mr. Welles. He is a clever fellow, indeed I have seen several of his screen appearances . . . his likeness reminds me of my late brother, Mycroft, and from what I have heard from you, and from other sources, they share certain characteristics. Now if you had a letter of introduction from Mycroft you would immediately be hired by the film magnate.' The conversation had made me fetch the envelope addressed to Lyle Garrison. Holmes smiled slyly as he said, 'You have not read the letter?' 'Why no, it is not intended for my eyes.' 'But it would help you to know what is said concerning you in the letter, would it not?' I was a little shocked at his suggestion. 'It would, but steaming and resealing an envelope usually makes it rather obvious that one has done so.' 'I agree, but there are other ways of reading the letter without disturbing the seal.' I shrugged, 'How?' He replied, 'A foolish question really, but can you obtain a very thin pair of hair curling tongs?' I said that I thought I might manage to buy such an implement from Selfridges or Harrods, if not from some more nearby shop. I had complete faith in him and unquestioningly I went out and managed to purchase the tongs from a large chemists near the corner of Baker Street and George Street. I returned in triumph brandishing my purchase. Holmes directed operations. I was to insert the implement into the space between the top edge of the envelope and the gummed flap. He said, 'Can you do this so that the actual letter is trapped between the two arms of the tongs?' It took a quarter of an hour but in the end I managed it. He continued, 'Good. Now turn the instrument as if you were curling hair. In doing this you will wind the letter tightly round the tongs. If you are careful you will be able to remove the letter from the envelope along with the business portion of the tongs.' He was right. I lost grip several times but as I repeated it I managed to remove the rolled letter without tearing the flap. I straightened it out and read it aloud.

My Dear Lyle,

This is to introduce my friend, Mr. Greg Hargreaves, with whose work you are doubtless familiar. I have long admired his script writing and have felt that he deserved better things than those he has been engaged upon here in the States. He has a story outline to show you which, I feel sure, will interest you as much as it does your humble servant. Should you decide to take an option at least on his script, I would consider very seriously playing the leading role should my commitments make this humanly possible.

I may be in London in a few weeks time and will give you a call.

Love to Rosalie and the kids,

Sincerely,
Orson Welles

The letter now presented me with two major problems. First, what on earth was this story outline to be. (My past employment had entailed my working on existing story lines). Second, and of more immediate importance, how the heck was I going to get the letter back into its envelope. Holmes told me how to do so.

'It's just a reversal of what you have already done. Wind the letter tightly around the tongs and reinsert. Withdraw the tongs and shake the envelope around. The letter will soon resume its former position with a little coaxing. Then roll and unroll the envelope with the letter inside which will destroy the evidence.'

Holmes had approved of what Orson had written saying, 'A clever epistle, with an element of blackmail in the hint of the offer of his own celebrated presence in the film. I feel sure that this Mr. Lyle Garrison will consider kindly this script as I believe you call it.' I nodded dumbly, 'Yes, but I do wish Orson had mentioned to me that I was supposed to show up with some kind of a script. I don't have a word on paper. I was really looking for an adaptation job, based on someone else's book.' He said, 'Well, we will have to get to work, will we not? Come, Hargreaves, the game is afoot. Get out your typewriting machine and charge the clay, as even the outline will surely be a three-pipe operation!'

I cannot say how very honoured and grateful I felt towards this enterprising apparition. It is not every crime writer, and none since Conan Doyle, that could truthfully claim that Sherlock Homes aided him. I sat with my Remington charged with quarto paper and the clay charged with 'Scottish Mixture', but for the first time in years without a constructive idea in my head. He sensed my uncertainty. 'Make a start, Hargreaves, and the rest will follow. Type something . . . anything . . . ' I rattled off the words 'OUTLINE FOR A CRIME STORY' in capitals. Then I underlined the words and brought the paper into a suitable position for those first tentative words. He asked, 'What is of first importance; the crime that is to be solved, or he who solves it? I imagine that everything is in the characterisation is it not, as with Chesterton's *Father Brown*? At the cinema I have seen films about detectives and always they seemed to have some other occupation as well. For instance *The Thin Man* was also a novelist, and that little Japanese chap was also an antique dealer and so on. The public as far as I can see are pleased with this arrangement. Have your detectives in your past work been amateurs?' I said, 'Sometimes when they were not Inspector this or that. Usually I have had to follow another's format.' He grunted, 'Well you are on your own now are you not?' But this was not quite true, for I had the assistance of the greatest of all detectives.

I said, 'O.K., Mr. Holmes, so first I must find an occupation for our detective. Of course, it does not have to be his livelihood. It could be his hobby. For instance he could be a taxidermist or a philatelist.' He said, 'I like the philatelist better. You are on the right lines, but how about a more active hobby or sport, such as archery for instance?' Inspiration hit me smack in the middle of the forehead,

'How about an angler?' 'Ah, (Holmes was impressed) now you have it, Hargreaves! An angler has a lot of time for contemplation and if he is a good one his mind would work in just the right fashion for an amateur sleuth. What will you call him?' I was inspired now, 'Isaac Walton?' 'Walton certainly, but if you call him Isaac he will be too near to the original, *The Complete Angler* himself. How about Septimus Walton, *The Complete Investigator?*' My index fingers worked overtime, 'He needs a friend. Some one that he can discuss his investigation with . . . his Watson if you like.' 'Ah, yes, very sound. He would need to be a little less shrewd, but only a very little. Someone who might go fishing with him on a regular basis. Perhaps the local vicar.' I warmed to his theme. He could throw up his hands and say 'Upon my word Walton, you are verily a fisher of evil men!'

Within half an hour I had tapped out the bare bones of what I considered to be a first class mystery story. As I typed, Holmes had marched up and down, occasionally stooping to see what had been typed and to take a deep lung full of the pipe smoke. Whenever he thought I was going wrong, he would point an accusing finger at the page and look questioningly at me.

In this way we produced an adventure for Septimus Walton and his colleague, the Reverend Henry McCombe. It concerned a certain Lord Witherspoon who each quarter organised a fishing contest in a local lake. His Lordship always won, catching the largest fish, all the others being returned to the pool. It was recognised that His Lordship would always win, the other contestants deliberately losing to him. This was because he would weigh his fish and give a correspondingly heavy sum of money to local causes. One of the conditions of the contest was that the pool should be fished only on the same days each year with the local police guarding it carefully at all other times. All went well until one of the villagers, less respectful than the rest, actually won the contest and insisted on keeping his fish. However, before he could get it to the taxidermist, it was stolen from him. He took his story to Walton, knowing him to be not only a keen angler, but also something of a criminologist. Walton and his friend McCombe decided to enter the contest at the next opportunity to enable them to investigate. The puzzle thus presented was all my own work.

Holmes approved of it, saying, 'Come, you are a fellow after my own heart. Now let us investigate and try to solve the case for your detective. Why, Hargreaves, is His Lordship so determined to win a contest which he has himself inaugurated, and why would anyone want to steal the winning fish and what type of fish is it?'

I said, 'It had better be a carp for they grow very large and are as edible as fresh water fish ever are. There again, maybe it should be a trout for they are even more of a delicacy.' Holmes put his foot down, 'No, you were right the first time, for trout only occur in fast running streams and this is a pool.' I agreed and said, 'As for the value of the giant carp, I feel that it ought to be down to something that the fish had swallowed.' Holmes was impressed, 'Excellent, but what?' 'Jewellery?' He nodded, 'Good idea. Now the jewellery has either been inserted into the fish, or been swallowed by it. What bait would you use for carp fishing? I no longer have my albums and books.' Fortunately I knew the answer. 'Bread paste, and hey, you could mould a gem or two into such a ball of dough so that it could be swallowed by a big fish and be retained in its gut!' I was quite excited now. Holmes was more restrained, 'But why would anyone want to feed these valuable pellets to the fish and have them retain the gemstones?' I rejoined, 'To hide them following their theft.' Holmes shook his head, 'His Lordship is hardly likely to be a jewel thief. He is far more likely to be the victim of a robbery.' Inspiration came to me, 'Suppose the family jewels had been stolen, but were heavily insured, and so the old boy was able to restore the family fortunes with the insurance money?' Holmes said, 'Brilliant. He could have fed the fish in the local pond with the jewel loaded bread paste with a view to getting them back gradually through the years. He has to stop others from catching them and hence the contest and its rules. Upon my word, what are the landed gentry coming to, Hargreaves?' I asked, 'Would it be feasible for the locals to be decent enough to let the old boy win every time?' He said, 'When you have been here a little longer, my dear Hargreaves, you will understand our rural ways of life. The Lord of the Manor is all-powerful, or at least he was until fairly recent times. Remember to set your story in a slightly earlier period, 1923 or so, as that would make it believable. Well you have the almost perfect crime.' I pondered, 'A little bit hard to swallow, don't you think, Mr. Holmes?' He chuckled, '*The Strand* readers never ever raised the slightest objection to far more unlikely events presented by Watson through Sir Arthur! My reappearance several years after plunging to my death at the Reichenbach Falls took a bit of believing. Well, you have your mystery, Hargreaves, and its explanation. All you need now is to tell your audience how Walton solved it.'

After more industrious work on the typewriter I had constructed Walton's curtain speech in which he laid everything out for his open-mouthed listeners. The theft of the winning fish, along with the discovery of a small gem in another fish that he had himself hooked, told him most of the answers to the riddle. Some research via the local newspapers of earlier years had turned up the news story concerning the jewel robbery at Witherspoon Towers. All I needed now was the outcome. Was Lord Witherspoon to be marched away to the cells or could more be extracted from the situation. Holmes had the last word, as usual. 'His Lordship, having speculated with the insurance money had again become wealthy enough to return the payment to the insurance company. The local police would have been placated by his promise that the fishing contest could be a fair one in which he would not even take part! Don't screw your face up like that, Hargreaves, it is only a story!'

While Holmes rested, I threw the hastily typed notes into some sort of professional looking synopsis. Then I typed out a couple of actual scenes for a screen play so that Garrison would realise that I meant business. Since I do not belong to the W. C. Fields 'synopsis on a cigarette packet' school, I broadened the outline to include a couple of sub plots, with extra incidents, and characters encountered, at the fishing inn where Walton and McCombe were staying. As a 'once in a while' contest would hardly make such an enterprise possible, I placed my inn on the river, a few miles from Witherspoon Towers, making additional scenes and characters quite natural and feasible. After an all night session, I figured that I had the outline of a full length detective adventure movie. All the elements were there. I even introduced the obligatory love interest by having a *femme fatale* as the driving force behind Lord Witherspoon, egging him on to do wrong. I kept quiet about some of my script developments assuming that Holmes might disapprove.

I slept for perhaps two hours, washed, shaved and then started to easy over a couple of eggs. Holmes joined me and sat at the table opposite as I ate. He said, 'Watson was always a late riser too.' I said warmly, 'Yes, but Watson probably slept more than two hours at a stretch.' He nodded wisely, 'Putting a few finishing touches to our masterpiece. Eh, Hargreaves! When are you going to present it to the great man along with friend Welles' letter of introduction?' There being no telephone at Hudson House, I told him that I would need to use a nearby booth. He said, 'There is a telephone kiosk almost opposite, Hargreaves. It was not there in my day. I had retreated to Fowlhaven by the time that particular instrument of torture had become universal. I never cared for the telephone, but Mycroft quite took to it, conducting all his business on it and having even less reason to leave the Diogenes Club.'

Managing to reach Lyle Garrison on the telephone, I found that the mention of Orson's letter of introduction ensured me of at least an interview and a fair hearing. Back home you can always get to see the 'top banana' even if he only gives you three minutes. Only in Europe is it so difficult to get to see people. I guess a lot of good work and talent falls by the wayside in consequence.

My appointment was for the following morning and I took a train to Aylesbury from Marylebone station. An aged taxi took me from the station to the premises of Buckinghamshire De Luxe Pictures. I alighted at the entrance to an old mansion of the kind that, in a 'Lithograph' movie, would have elicited a 'No-one goes *there*' from the cabbie. My feet scrunched on the gravel drive and I rang the bell, half expecting Peter Lorre or John Carradine to answer the door. Instead, no one answered and I realised that the door was unlocked. There was a reception desk just inside. The uniformed receptionist surprised me because he was white. (Back home he would have been black almost for certain, even in the fifties. I remember thinking, 'Gee, they have poor whites over here just like in the deep south?' but I am now ashamed at the thought). I gave him my name and told him of my appointment with Lyle

Garrison. He gave me one of those glances that only British working people can manage, as if to say, 'Oh yes, I can just imagine him wanting to see *you*!' He did something clever with a switchboard, held some muttered conversation and then smiled at me begrudgingly and pointed to a flight of stairs saying, 'up the steps, sir, and first on the left at the top.' I stood there gazing at the marble staircase which looked for all the world as if it had been built by Universal Studios for Bela Lugosi to stand atop to make his 'Children of the night how sweetly they *sing*!' speech. I reached the landing and found the framed oak door with Lyle Garrison's shield on it.

The great man proved to be terribly un-theatrical, even by British standards. He was small, he was bald and he was podgy. He spoke with an accent that to my untrained ear could have been anything but that of the South of England. Had Holmes been with me, he could have told me the town, and even perhaps the district of the town, from which Garrison came. (I had not brought

48

Holmes with me because I realised that he, as a ghost, might have been anti-sales!)

The little guy read Orson's letter eagerly, then he smiled and said, 'Such a clever man, if only he was more co-operative he would be a star rather than an artistic institution. You have a synopsis for me? Good! Tell me, is there a suitable part for Orson. One important enough for him to accept, but small enough for its filming not to stretch his attention span? You know what he is like! He loves to arrive, do a couple of days work, cop the money and blow!' I chuckled nervously, 'Yes, there is a wonderful cameo role for him (I wracked my brain in panic and fortunately came up with the answer to a question that I had forgotten to ask myself) the part of Lord Witherspoon.' He was impressed, 'Great, he plays lords and kings so well. If it is a Scottish laird so much the better because he has played one for us before and we still have his costume.' He started to read my synopsis and I was happy to note that his lips did not move as he did so.

Like an actor auditioning his talent, the writer, waiting whilst his work is being read, is experiencing his worst nightmare. I have never figured out the right manner to adopt during such a nerve-wracking interlude. Should one sit back casually, as if either confident of the outcome or independent enough not to care, or adopt an enthusiastic air of expectation, leaning towards the reader in one's chair? I just sat and recited speeches from Hamlet in my head, trying to pretend that this was not a really important moment in my life. After what seemed like an age, he looked up and gave me his thoughts upon that which he had been reading.

'Greg, it's a great piece of characterisation and a great theme for a television series rather than a film.' Sensing my instant disappointment, he raised a hand as if it would stop me from saying anything. It did. He continued, 'This is a stroke of luck for both of us, Greg. You see we are expanding into television. Of course, we will continue to make movies, but the real future is with the square eyed little monster in everybody's living room.

It happens that I have to present a prospectus of projects to our backers shortly. Now, I'll tell you what I want to do. I want to be able to show them half a dozen outlines for a new television series that we have first refusal on. I'd like your angling detective, Walton, to be among the properties that I have on offer. This means that I can't promise anything regarding the future of the series because it's not only my say so, but I'm confident that it will interest my backers and fellow directors.'

My heart sank, remembering my early days back home where I had been encouraged by such words only to be plunged into miserable disappointment later. Moreover, I needed some money, for despite my modest rent, I had brought so little of anything with me from the land of opportunity that I would soon be counting my dollars a bit anxiously. However, I was cheered a little by his next words, 'I can arrange a small payment to you by taking an option on the series . . . perhaps a thousand pounds?' I swiftly translated the pounds into dollars in my

51

SPRINGDALE PUBLIC LIBRARY
105 South Pleasant
Springdale, Arkansas 72764

head and nodded, smiling, as I realised that it would get me out of trouble for months rather than weeks. We shook hands on the promise of an option contract being prepared and eventually signed.

I returned to Baker Street, not exactly elated but vastly relieved. I had one foot on the lowest rung of the British entertainment ladder, and the fiend McCarthy had not even needed to be mentioned. Britain was drab and had barely recovered from the most terrible war in history. Bomb debris still lay around and there were shortages in the stores, but I sensed an overwhelming *sanity* prevailing in a land where everyone still seemed to expect life to be fair. It was refreshing to be gaped at in the street for wearing a fringed leather jacket after dwelling so long in a place where there seemed little point in dressing ever so slightly outrageously if no one ever seemed surprised.

Holmes gave me a shrewd glance from the sofa upon which he was elegantly laid. He said, 'Well, Hargreaves, I deduce that your errand has been not altogether unproductive even if it did not reach the goal for which you had aimed.' I asked, 'You deduced that from my manner?' He said, 'That and other things. So your angling detective is to become a star of the airwaves rather than of the silver screen.' I admit that I was taken aback asking, 'How could you know a thing like that unless you have powers of invisibility of which you have kept me in ignorance?' He chuckled, 'My dear Hargreaves, you entered the room and as you laid down your briefcase you rather thoughtfully looked at the wireless set in the corner of the room, and your expression changed from one of modest triumph to one of shrugging acceptance. The wireless has been there for years, but it is the first time that you have looked at it long and hard since your arrival at these rooms, though I'll wager you have been aware of it all along.' He was so nearly right and his deductive train so brilliant that I hardly liked to make the minor correction. 'Wonderful, Holmes, you astound me. As it happens the character may become a regular feature of television but the airwaves still apply.' He frowned, 'Of course, and in the absence of such an instrument you looked for the wireless which was the nearest thing to it. I am getting out of touch you see, for although I have long been aware of Baird's invention, one seldom sees it when in my situation. I do not often enter people's homes because it has such a frightening effect upon anyone that I may encounter. One sees it being demonstrated in electrical shop windows, but it is so small and flickers so much that I am quite surprised that it is a medium wealthy enough to pay you a fair price for our little joint effort. By the way, you may take my part of the payment in return for any expenses that I have caused you to incur.'

I switched on the radio (as I had been raised to call it) and having adjusted it suitably, I started to get a clear signal from one of the stations. I turned the volume down and left it on in the background because the light music was pleasant enough. Holmes started to tap his foot and his fingers twitched as if playing an invisible violin. I was suddenly filled with compassion for this brilliant man who would never again be able to play an instrument which had always given him so much pleasure. As ever he read my mind, 'Come, Hargreaves, it is not so bad really. After all I can go to concerts whenever I please. In recent years I have heard Campoli, Kreisler and the young Menuhin. Would that I had managed to find the time to fall under the spell of the great violin virtuosos of former days. It was possible, occasionally, but all too often I would be required to change my plans at the very last minute. Also, Watson, although a really splendid fellow, and no man could ask for a more loyal friend, was just not musical and I could never hold his attention for long when playing upon my own instrument, unless I played Strauss or some other undemanding composer. I suppose you will be installing a television instrument soon?' I noted a touch of curiosity in his enquiry, although doubtless it was meant to be made in a tone of contempt. I said,

'I am thinking of doing so.' He nodded, his sharp features assuming a long-suffering expression.

On the following morning in the mail, I received from Lyle Garrison a letter and an option contract with a duplicate to sign and return. As I read the letter, Holmes peered over my shoulder. It was an action that I could scarcely resent considering his involvement. He said, 'You are dealing with a company which has, or at least has had, considerable capital if their outlay upon this printed item is to be taken into account. Notice the die sunk lettering allied to heavy enamel printing ink. An extremely costly process, and it has been used upon the finest quality paper. Hold it up to the light . . . ah, yes, the watermark is just what I would have expected. The typing has been done with a modern and well-maintained machine. Notice how clean the type is, and the ribbon used is of equally fine quality. Now look at the top line of print and read it aloud.' I read, 'Buckingham De Luxe Pictures and Television Features'. He said, 'Notice that the words 'and Television Features' has been added to the existing letter-head, but skilfully I'll grant you. You can see from the sheen on the printing ink that it is glossier on the second line as it has been more recently printed. A fly-by-night organisation would have simply added an adhesive strip, and would not have gone to the expense of overprinting an already expensive letter head.'

I perused the contract fairly carefully, but was inclined to just sign and return it in my relief. However, I decided to ask Holmes to have a look at it as an interested party. I spread it on the table, turning and placing it suitably as he directed, holding my spare spectacles a few inches above so that the once gimlet eyed, but more recently myopic, detective could read it. He nodded grimly asking, 'What do you make of it, Hargreaves?' I said, 'It is standard of its kind, nothing for me to seriously question. I'm rather relieved that Garrison appears to be quite unaware of my problem with friend McCarthy. Orson did not mention it in the letter and neither did he in conversation.'

Holmes dropped what at that moment was a minor bombshell. He said, 'Oh, yes, Hargreaves, he is very well aware of your problem. Look at clause sixteen and read it very carefully.' I turned to the clause that he mentioned and read it, questioningly, aloud, 'In the event of the series being shown in the United States of America, the writer will raise no unreasonable objection to another name being used in the screen credits.'

So, Holmes was right and Lyle Garrison really did know of my brush with McCarthy. I said, 'Well, as he does know I suppose the clause is understandable really. After all, he is going to sink a lot of capital into 'Walton'. At least, we hope he is. He would not want to lose the American market just because my name would not win a political popularity contest. Do you not think, upon reflection, that I should just sign and accept the inevitable?' Holmes, as I have already remarked and exemplified, had lost none of his shrewdness, and gave me a fresh example of this. 'In accepting his clause, Hargreaves, you might wish to insert one of your own, to the effect that you agree for a name other than your own to be used, but that you reserve the right to choose the name yourself.' I was puzzled, 'What would be the advantage to me in this, Holmes? If I choose to be called William Shakespeare Jones, only you and I will know who the writer really is and the great viewing public will be none the wiser.' He smiled and raised a long thin finger, 'Ah, but if the name that you chose were to be Gregory Hathaway Hargreaves, rather than Greg Hargreaves, the terms of the contract would be met and anyone who knows of you would see through the deception.' I didn't know if I could get away with it, but I figured the ruse was worth a try. I typed a letter to that effect and posted it back to Garrison requesting new copies of the contract with that amendment. I was taking a chance, but it was, Holmes agreed, a chance worth taking.

This proved to be so and even if Garrison saw through the ruse he chose to accept it and I signed and mailed him a copy of the amended agreement a few days later. Holmes nodded wisely at the news of this, saying, 'Even the wicked Senator would be forced to accept the situation. He dare not push his power beyond a certain stage lest his credulity be taken a little too far. In any case, he may not even have his attention drawn to the matter.'

Cheques (I have learned to stop calling them 'checks') from film companies and television people have a habit of taking far longer to materialise than at first expected, and the one from Buckinghamshire De Luxe was no exception. But it did materialise not much more than a week beyond my expectation. Not bad for movie people. Holmes remarked, 'A good sign the slight delay, because you can wager it was caused by their legal persons giving the new clause their attention. If you are in funds now, Hargreaves, you might treat me to a night out at the theatre.' This request surprised me, 'Surely you can go to the theatre whenever you wish. Have you not told me as much?' He said, 'Yes, but only to sneak in and claim an unsold seat. It would be nice to be there by right just for once. There is a new play, a mystery, by Agatha Christie that has just opened. I have long admired her writings, Hargreaves, especially those that concern her little Belgian detective and his Watson of a friend. She has a clever way of surprising and deceiving her audience by making the criminal the least suspicious character. Her plotting is a work of art, Hargreaves, however contrived. As a crime writer you should remember that the public will accept the most unlikely twist in the tail so long as it is logical and entertainingly presented.'

Sherlock Holmes travelled with me in a taxicab to the theatre despite his need of transport being minimal! He, of course, presented a rather bizarre picture with his gaunt grey face, red dressing gown and deerstalker. For the first, and perhaps only, time during our association, I wished that invisibility could have been one of his ghostly talents. As it was, I explained to the cab driver and the theatre usher, 'He has been very ill, but so wanted to see the play.' The first act of the play I found entertaining enough, approving of the way in which Mrs. Christie introduced and developed her characters. The first act curtain fell upon the discovery of Lord Sunley, shot dead in the library. During the ensuing interval Holmes ruined my enjoyment of the rest of the piece by telling me who would logically be the murderer. Had he left it at that it might not have been a completely wasted evening, but in addition he told me whom Mrs. Christie would be certain to nominate for the role of killer in the final minutes of the play. I thought perhaps it would be the butler as the 'least likely'. 'No, he's *too* 'least likely', Hargreaves. The man who called distributing the religious tracts is your man. If you examine the plot you will find that he has been introduced solely for the purpose of providing a murderer. His reason for killing Lord Sunley probably had to be contrived at the very last minute, but you will see that she will tie up all the details in a most orderly and believable fashion ... I'll wager the motive will be quite trivial. In real life, murders fall into two categories; spur of the moment killings that present no mystery, and the murder that is planned. The latter will subdivide into the hastily planned killing that will be easy to solve, and the killing which is planned by some one with a good, if evil, brain and will present the detective with a problem.'

Holmes was, of course, right about the identity of the killer. It was all logical enough in the end, even when the tract distributor was still there to be accused just before the final curtain. Mrs. Christie had contrived this by creating a situation where the characters were all unable to leave the crime scene through freak weather conditions making them all conveniently available for the last act. The murderer had presumably managed to arrive just before the storm reached its worst excesses. As a fellow writer of detective fiction I naturally defended the play and its construction over a pipe back at Baker Street.

I asked, 'Were there not cases, real

ones, in which you took part where similarly contrived outcomes occurred?' He shook his head, 'No, Hargreaves. Let us consider what has been generally considered to be my most famous case . . . that which Watson and Doyle decided to title *The Hound of the Baskervilles.* (Sir Henry Baskerville was, of course, a name contrived to protect his privacy). Had Mrs. Christie been writing the case as a fiction, I have no doubt that Frankland, unlovable in his obsession with bringing lawsuits, and suspicious through his use of his telescope, would have turned out to be the criminal. Twists and turns could have been added to the facts, and he, or even Doctor Mortimer, could have been a convincing culprit. In a real life drama, such as that, which had Dartmoor as its backdrop, those with absolutely no motive would hardly have committed the crime. No, the real would be murderer turned out to be someone with an excellent motive, and in Watson's documentation he at no time hid any fact that might have led his reader to suspect Stapleton. All the facts were there,

Hargreaves, and all were lovingly spread upon a huge table for the reader to devour and decide upon. The climax *was* a surprise to most who read the chapters, but should not have been! It was only a surprise on account of their inability to make deductions from the facts presented and not through any attempt to conceal anything from them. Of course, this was all based upon fact, but good fiction should imitate fact should it not?'

It was on the following morning that the television set arrived and was installed. It had a rather small screen by American standards, but Holmes found it fascinating, especially the news bulletins and documentary programmes. Of course, when I went out I would leave it on for him, but he was naturally unable to turn it off and I would sometimes return to find him seated as far from the instrument as he could manage and facing the window, when the programme was not to his liking. Sometimes he was forced to leave the room through a sudden variation in the volume, or on one occasion to leave the building entirely during a programme of loud modern music, though on the whole, the installation was a success for Holmes had found little opportunity to enjoy this new medium in the past. He was a ghost and as such could go anywhere he wished. But even a ghost can be a gentleman.

'Hargreaves, how could I possibly suddenly appear in some family circle whilst they were watching their favourite programme? I only tried it once, with the result that dogs barked, children screamed and women fainted. If only I could become invisible at will, but that would be too much to ask I suppose. Come, I should not complain of my lot, for I am left with possibilities far beyond the expectations of an agnostic! What are you cooking tonight? I'll wager that *soufflé* of Philip Harben's would have a fine aroma?'

It was whilst we watched a biographical feature concerning Charles Dickens that an idea hit me right bang smack in the centre of my brain. Once more, Sherlock Holmes surprised me by reading my mind. 'True, Hargreaves, the life and times of Sherlock Holmes could make an excellent television programme.' I made to protest my surprise at his knowing what had crossed my mind, but he raised a weary hand saying, 'Oh, please, if I have scored a bull's eye it is more by luck than judgement on this occasion. You looked very thoughtful during the latter part of the biographical entertainment, and you several times cast a calculating glance in my direction. It was not a deduction but a calculated guess. You see I have broken my own golden rule.'

I said, 'I admit that the thought was there, Holmes, but there is one large fly in the ointment. Most people are under the impression that you are purely a fictional character, and that both Watson and yourself were figments of Sir Arthur Conan Doyle's vivid imagination. This flame has been well and truly fanned through the years by impersonations of you. First there was William Gillette, and later Messrs. Barrymore, Brook, Wontner and Rathbone.' Holmes chuckled, 'Gillette was too heavily built, whilst Barrymore was far too handsome, and

Brook was too stolid. Wontner was nearer, but Rathbone was the best of my imitators. If only he had been served with better stories, Hargreaves, he could have been quite perfect. Had you and I formed an alliance at an earlier date, it could have been very helpful for Mr. Rathbone.'

Whilst Holmes rested upon his bed in the nearest imitation of sleep available to him, I burnt the midnight oil. 'Sherlock Holmes, Fact or Fiction?' I already had the title for a documentary that could make my name on British television. As for the research, I had access to most of it without leaving my rooms, in the shape of Sherlock Holmes, the 'Ghost of Baker Street'.

3

'Hargreaves, what on earth is that?'

It was a few days later and Holmes had suddenly materialised following a brisk walk in Regent's Park. As he spoke he gesticulated in the direction of an instrument that stood in the centre of the breakfast table, its accessories occupying most of the space that remained upon the green cloth.

'It is a Grundig tape recording machine Holmes, and, as you can see, it has a vast length of magnetic tape mounted upon two large spools. The tape runs through a recording head, rather after the style of moving picture film through a camera or projector. If I turn it on thus, it will record what I am saying onto the tape, so that I can later reverse it, run it back and listen to what I have said. When I was in Hollywood we used something similar but it worked on magnetic wire rather than a tape.' Holmes took all this in very calmly saying, 'So it produces a soundtrack rather like a moving picture camera does for talkies. Of course, it is not entirely a new invention, because I can remember many years ago, a machine called a 'dictaphone' that performed a similar function. One spoke into a tube that copied one's speech onto a cylinder, rather like Edison's early 'phonograph', but I can see that this machine is more sophisticated and uses a microphone as in broadcasting. Does one need a fresh reel of the tape for each recording made?' I explained, 'You can keep it and use a fresh one if it is what you want. If not you can reuse the tape as often as you wish. You can stop and start it at the touch of a button. It has disadvantages in being rather cumbersome and heavy, but I have no doubt that time will bring improvements.'

Holmes nodded shrewdly, 'I can see what a useful machine it could be for the recording of information. Had it been available half a century ago it would have saved me a lot of storage problems, and made it easier for Mrs. Hudson to dust the room. Some persons might purchase this instrument to use as a toy, Hargreaves, especially if they enjoyed the sound of their own voice, but you are not childish, nor yet egotistical, and therefore the instrument is here to help you with your profession. We discussed the possibility a few days ago of you writing a biographical documentary concerning myself. (So many people use the expression 'your humble servant' for self referral, but as I am far from humble and nobody's servant, I never do). I could recount my life story into the microphone. Later you could play it back in sections so that you could type it at your own speed. That is to over simplify, but basically true?'

'Yes, I cannot deny it, but I would only proceed with such a plan with your complete co-operation. The machine is too large to hide and so I could not secretly record anything, even if I wished to do so. You have only to say so and I will drop the whole idea. After all, the recorder will be useful to me in other ways.' I charged the clay with tobacco as he sat in deep thought. I lit it with the Zippo and puffed as much smoke in his direction as my lungpower would permit. He grunted and said, 'I will indeed co-operate with you, Hargreaves, but only under certain conditions. First, you must use the recording only for your own convenience in transferring my words to the typed page. Second, in your writing of the biography, you will give me complete editorial control, which I believe to be the modern journalistic term?'

It had crossed my mind that his voice, being not from one who is of this world, might not record at all. Later, having allowed him to give me a brief concise account of his early life and career, I was happy to find that all was well. I rewound the tape and pushed the play button to be rewarded by those rather high, intense tones that were unmistakable. 'I was born in January of 1854 to a family of English country squires . . . '

You know, it's a strange thing, but however honest, well meaning and straightforward one is, or considers oneself to be, there will always come a time when the temptation to perform some act of treachery is too strong to resist. There is a more than selfish streak in all of us and I suddenly realised that I had to weigh my friendship with the 'Baker Street Ghost' against possible fame, fortune and even immortality. For if I, Greg Hargreaves, were to produce this apparition of Sherlock on tape, film, or even on television, I would be more than just a crime writer, more than merely a famous one, and even Joe McCarthy would be happy to own me as the American citizen that I was. Holmes realised, of course, that I was wrestling with a problem in my mind, but even his shrewd powers of observation could not deduce its exact nature. Whatever his thoughts on the matter, he made no allusion to my possible state of mind.

I phoned Lyle Garrison at Buckinghamshire De Luxe from a call booth at Baker Street station, rather than risk the nearer one, and I made quite sure that

Holmes did not appear to be around. Maybe I did, for the first time in my life, play the heavy salesman when I told him that I was on to something for which any film company in the world would give their eye-teeth. I'm sure I overplayed my hand, but then I had never had such a hand to play before. He sounded calm but made an appointment for me to come right over and see him. (I refused, politely, to enlighten him further over the phone).

Whilst Holmes took what passed for a nap, I changed the tape on the Grundig, replacing it, of course, with one that looked identical, safe in the knowledge that Holmes could not operate the machine in my absence. With his biographical tape in my briefcase, I left for Aylesbury, Buckinghamshire De Luxe and the anticipation of world celebrity!

Lyle Garrison greeted my halting oration concerning the 'Ghost of Baker Street' with a nervous amusement. I could tell that he hoped I was kidding him. He said, 'A great idea for a story,

Greg, and I can understand your enthusiasm which prompts, shall I say, 'theatricals'? Why don't you rough it out and let me consider it. After all, we've got 'Walton', the angling detective, to think about first.' I was slightly exasperated, 'You don't get me, do you? This is no story line that I am telling you about, this is the ghost of Sherlock Holmes in his old Baker Street setting. It's the greatest true story in the world and will forever answer the enigma concerning the possibility of an afterlife! If you are not interested, I'll take it some place else.'

Garrison was truly nervous now. I had said too much, too soon. He was optically measuring his distance from the door (unless my sojourn with Holmes had made me mistake his intentions). Then suddenly he relaxed. Evidently the suspicion of my being dangerously crazy, or at least partially so, had passed. He spoke kindly, as if to an excitable horse or dog, 'Take it easy, Greg, I can tell that you are serious in what you say. Well, O.K., but it's a pity you don't have some kind of proof. Not that I doubt your word, but could you not have been hoodwinked . . . or just plain mistaken about all this? Greg, let me mull this over, you know you should take your character Walton's advice and do a little fishing.' As he rose from his chair I played what I thought might be my trump card and slipped my tape onto his machine saying, 'Just listen to this, Lyle, then I'll leave you in peace if you want me to.' He sank back rather unwillingly.

'I was born in 1854 to a family of English country squires . . . '

He listened to the concise clipped speech for a while and I could see uncertainty eventually taking the place of disbelief in his expression. I switched it off and then hit the rewind button. As the tape whirred he said, 'O.K., Greg, it sounds kosher enough, but how can I be sure from just a sound recording. I would have to see this phenonemon for myself, even film it.' To cut a rather long interview short, he agreed to call upon me at noon on the following day, at which time I was reasonably convinced that the

'Ghost of Baker Street' would be at home, if the recent past could be relied upon.

On my way back to Baker Street I convinced myself that I would be able to placate Holmes when Garrison called, planning to pass him off as a friend with a problem. I would then introduce Holmes as an old friend or relative without mention of his supernatural character. As I practised to deceive I was weaving a web in which I would need to be careful not to become enmeshed myself.

On the morning that followed I arose early, for me, to find that Holmes had already departed upon some errand of his own which he had given no hint of on the night before, but I had no reason to believe that he would not return in good time to participate in my devious plan. It was not until eleven had turned into eleven thirty that I began to worry just a little. When Lyle Garrison arrived promptly at noon I was indeed concerned about the non-appearance of Sherlock Holmes. I seated him in the most comfortable chair, from which he would be the first to see Holmes' dramatic return, giving him a drink, but failing in my attempts at small talk.

He looked around anxiously enquiring, 'Is he here now?' I tried to explain that Holmes did not have the gift of invisibility. 'You will see him!' I said, optimistically adding some details, 'He will look like a living person save in the abrupt manner of his arrival.' He tried to make light of it, 'Now you don't see him, now you do, eh?' I chuckled dutifully and said, 'I can't think what is keeping him, he enjoys a pipe of his special 'Scottish Mixture' at about this time . . . by proxy.' I filled a clay, lit it and puffed out the blue smoke. Garrison coughed, and his expression showed a glint of understanding. He enquired, 'This 'Scottish Mixture', is it some kind of dope?' I was hurt at his suggestion that the 'Ghost of Baker Street' had been some kind of hallucinatory phenomena. 'Certainly not!' By one thirty Sherlock Holmes had still failed to put in an appearance and Lyle was putting away his pocket watch and movie camera, and preparing to depart. As he donned his fedora he said, 'Greg, keep in touch, work on 'Walton' but don't overdo things, especially the 'Scottish Mixture'. Get plenty of sleep and it might do you no harm to visit a quack.'

I waited in vain for the return of the 'Ghost of Baker Street', my mood varying from guilt to self-pity and irritability. When by evening he had not re-appeared, I decided to forget everything and go out on the town.

In search of cheer I went to a bar in the Edgware Road, where there was a crowd of jolly Irish drinkers. I did not participate in their jollity, however, and in preferring the danger of being a lone tippler, I was following my own routine for getting well and truly sozzled. This I had established through the years for my very occasional alcoholic interludes. Other ruses were to start off in the very cheapest joint, working my way through medium priced hostelries and finishing up in a high-class place. This system cuts down on the expense and the risk of being rolled. So, following my own rules, I ended up in a rather smart looking bar right off Baker Street itself, and from where I figured I would not have too much trouble making it back to Hudson House no matter what state I was in.

It was as I entered this bar that I realised I had reached that dangerous stage of intoxication where far from spinning or fuzzing over, everything springs into crystal sharp focus. Sights and sounds had great clarity but seemed to be happening at a distance and to someone else! I struck up a conversation with a large, jolly, blonde lady and cared not if I ever saw or heard of the 'Ghost of Baker Street' ever again.

We exchanged superficial confidences. Then she said, 'You're an American aren't you? I like Yanks. Knew a lot of them during the war.' Her skirt hoisted by an inch or two as she shifted herself up onto a barstool. About thirty five, she looked pleasantly vulgar without being an obvious harlot despite the nylon gloss on her thighs that screamed for further exploration. Instead I caressed the arch of her back in a rather formal way. This prompted her to say, 'You're a real gent. I'll 'ave another gin.' When I told her that I was stopping currently in Baker Street her eyes grew round. 'Well, are'nt you gonna invite me back for a nightcap? He'll be closin' 'ere in a minnit.' I purchased a bottle of gin from the barman, who gave me a rather strange look, somewhere between pity and envy.

I felt good once we were out in the street and pointed towards Baker Street, and soon I became convinced that there was no seven foot wrestler in the offing. (After all I should have remembered that this was London and not L.A.). She had donned a beaver coat against the cold and I explored beneath it. She said, 'Wait until we get inside, you bad boy!' I chuckled and we made it to the top of the stairs to my Hudson House apartment. Inside she looked around with interest throwing off the beaver coat carelessly. 'Not posh, but I've seen worse.' She collapsed onto the sofa and I poured gin into a couple of glasses. I asked her, 'Say when?' and she said, 'Right after this drink!' She laughed hugely at her own joke, and then, as I attempted to help her to disrobe, it was she who stiffened suddenly.

She peered with disbelief over the top of the sofa at something I had not seen. It was the 'Ghost of Baker Street' gazing at us with a great deal of disapproval. She gasped, 'Who is the old geezer in the red dressing gown?' I said, 'Ignore him, he's nothing. He'll be gone in a minute. He's very good at disappearing.' She jumped up, clutching the beaver coat around her and hissed, 'You didn't tell me there was gonna be an audience. What are you, some kind of pervert?' She made for the door, her heels clip-clopped down the stairs and the front door slammed. I glared at Holmes saying, 'Thanks a lot, Holmes, you've really given me a day to remember!' Then I collapsed on the sofa and took a stiff gulp of gin without troubling with the nicety of a glass. Then as I lay back on the cushions the room started to revolve, with the last thing I clearly remember being the figure of Sherlock Holmes spinning over my head.

When I awoke it was my eyes that hurt the most, especially when I tried to move them. I crawled from the sofa and into the bathroom where I worked hard for ten minutes or so, trying to restore myself to some kind of normality. After I had washed, shaved and taken some seltzer, I felt almost human and remembered from past experience that my recovery would be swift. Four, maybe five, times in my life I had experienced something like this situation, but never before with psychic complications. Holmes was, I noticed, still around and I no longer cared that I had betrayed his trust. After all, had he not wreaked a terrible revenge? However, I soon decided that I at least owed him a polite explanation even if I did open it with an ironic note.

'Holmes, I trust you enjoyed making a complete fool of me?' He was as bright as a button and full of the joys of spring, 'On the contrary, Hargreaves, it was you who made yourself foolish in the eyes of the adventuress.' 'What did you call her, Holmes?' 'An adventuress. That is the most polite term that I can think of to describe her.' I had not come across the expression before. 'Well, you certainly made me look a jerk, just by appearing at the wrong moment.' It was his turn to ask for clarification, 'What is a jerk?' I told him, 'A twerp with an American accent.' He laughed almost kindly, 'You know you did rather ask for it, Hargreaves, because you broke my confidence without consultation, and then laid the blame upon me when you were made to look foolish. You deserved your embarrassment.' I realised now that he was talking about my awful experience with Lyle Garrison and asked, 'How did you know that I had ratted on you? You were conspicuous by your absence, but your deduction is correct.' He said, 'I noticed that you had changed the tape reel on your machine. Whilst I could not test this theory, my eyes told me that the slight imperfection on the original, otherwise identical, reel,

84

was no longer there. Further I could tell from your slightly devious manner that you were embarking upon something about which you did not wish to confide. I realised what you were planning, and whilst I could not really blame you, for, how can I put it, seeking your fortune at my expense, I, at the same time, did not wish to become a sort of freak show! You owe me an apology and an assurance that you will never indulge yourself in such a scheme at my expense again.'

I was happy that he had let me off so lightly and that he had not threatened to terminate our amalgamation, but then, Sherlock Holmes was, and is, even in his present ethereal state, a perfect gentleman and would prove a wonderful ally in a most difficult time for me that was yet to come.

'Hargreaves, would you be so kind as to obtain a copy of The Times for me?' It was an hour or so later and I had made a good recovery from my hangover so I could hardly refuse to perform an errand for a forgiving friend. I took myself off to the nearest paper store and purchased a copy of *The Times*, and an overpriced imported issue of *Variety* that I might see the latest movie gossip. Back at Hudson House I spread the sheets of the newspaper so that Holmes could peruse them, turning them when he wish me to do so. In between performing this chore, I snatched a quick glance here and there at *Variety*. Its brittle show-speak reminding me of the rat-race that I had pulled out of and made me feel that I had done the right thing in taking the Orsonian advice. Holmes would clear his throat to signify when he wanted the pages to be turned. His wise comments upon the various news items and other features of the newspaper illustrated that he was just about the most well informed ghost in history. Not for him the loud moaning or chain clanking of his kind. He said, 'Hargreaves, may I commend you to read the item on page three under the roman style headline?' I read the piece with growing interest and concern.

McCARTHY'S AIDE FOUND DEAD
London, June 5th 1951. Senator
Joseph McCarthy's assistant, Mr.
Lionel Craig, visiting London on
important business for the Senator,
has been found dead in his hotel
bedroom from strangulation. The
authorities are interviewing a number
of American nationals, resident in or
visiting London, whose names appear
upon a list of those scheduled for
investigation by Craig, concerning
their involvement in so called
un-American activities. A police sur-
geon has estimated the time of death
as near eleven o'clock on Tuesday
night.

Holmes spoke calmly, 'Good old
'*Thunderer*', facts without conjecture.' I
replied, not quite so calmly, 'My name
will almost certainly appear upon that list
of suspects!' He nodded, 'Oh, yes, but
there may be others whose names will
suggest far greater urgency than yours to
be avoiding Craig's attentions. Remember

the old saying, 'Trouble, no trouble until trouble troubles you'. That is not to say, of course, that you should not prepare yourself for any possible interest that the police may show in you.' I said, 'I guess you mean that I should start thinking in terms of an alibi? Well then, I have nothing more to worry about Holmes. After all you were here with me at around the hour in question.' Of course, almost as soon as I had uttered these words, I realised my error and his reply was scarcely needed. 'My dear Hargreaves, do you honestly mean to say that you are going to tell a sceptical policeman that you spent the evening with the ghost of a well know personality? It is not only a tall story but one in which I refuse to have any part. You realise, I am sure, that were my present situation made public knowledge, it would be difficult for me to follow any sort of normal peaceful activities. Whenever I appeared, women would scream and men would brandish their walking sticks. There might even be clergy reciting words of exorcism at me! No, I cannot help you in that respect, but rest assured that I will help you in an advisory capacity for you were not only here from about ten-forty onwards, but would hardly have been in a fit state to strangle anyone for quite some time before that.'

I brightened suddenly, 'There was that girl, Holmes, she could give me the alibi that I need.' He pondered, 'She could hardly be deemed the most reliable of character witnesses. She does not know you very well, nor you she. Moreover, she saw *me*, and that would mean that you would have to speak out on a subject upon which we have agreed to remain silent. She would not leave me out of the story, I'll be bound, and you might want to forgo the pleasure of explaining how you tried to embrace her in the presence of an elderly man in a dressing gown. No, forget about her, Hargreaves!' I said thoughtfully, 'I was conspicuous in the bar, several bars in fact.' He nodded, 'Ah, now that is a rather better line to pursue.'

4

Trouble did indeed trouble me, and even sooner than I might have expected. It came in the shape of a detective inspector from Scotland Yard and his sergeant. When they entered the sitting room, the 'Ghost of Baker Street' was nowhere to be seen. I really was on my own. Inspector Reynolds (such an English name — in L.A. he would have been a Hodiak or Poluski, or at the very least a Columbini or O'Reilly) was polite enough. 'Mr. Hargreaves, I am investigating the suspicious circumstances surrounding the death of a fellow countryman of yours, a Mr. Craig. Do you know the deceased?' 'No, nor had I heard of him until I read of his death in *The Times*.' 'But, you have heard of Senator Joseph McCarthy, his employer?' 'Why yes, but only because he is infamous.'

Reynolds raised an eyebrow at the word

'infamous' and I wished at once that I had not used it. 'But, Mr. Hargreaves, your name appeared upon a typed list of suspect American nationals to be investigated by Mr. Craig.' I asked warmly, 'Suspected of what?' He coughed, 'There you have me, but my guess is that they were suspected of being communists, or communist sympathisers, who had left America to avoid investigation.' I enquired, 'Would I have been bound by British law to submit to his investigations?' He was uncertain, 'Probably not.' I played what I though to be an at least useful card, 'Then why would I want to be rid of him?' He rounded on me swiftly, 'I had not planned to make any sort of an accusation, Mr. Hargreaves, I simply want to interview every person on the list in case one, or more, of them could contribute some useful information to help us with our enquiries. With this in mind, could you give me some idea of your movements last evening, say between ten and midnight?'

'I went out about six or so, and spent the evening in a number of bars.' 'You mean public houses? What was your intention in visiting these establishments?' 'I guess they were public, there were a lot of people in them, and my intention was to buy and consume liquor.' 'Well, that makes sense, Mr. Hargreaves. Did you come into contact with anyone who might remember seeing you?' 'The bar-keeper, maybe. I am an American so maybe other imbibers might remember me. There was a girl I was talking to . . . ' (I trailed off, realising that I had made a mistake). 'Someone you knew?' I was careful now, 'Why, no, she was just a dame . . . a girl on her own.' 'What time did you speak with her?' 'Oh, about five to ten.' 'Did you take her anywhere when the bar closed?' 'No (I started to tell lies at this point), I just bid her goodnight and came straight back here.' 'Can you name this girl?' 'Well, no.' 'But you can at least describe her?' 'Yes, she was a blonde, about thirty odd, and wearing a leopard skin coat (I continued to lie).' The sergeant was writing this down. He was an earnest young man, and threw in the odd question of his own. 'No one else could confirm your movements. I mean you don't share this large flat with anyone?' 'No, I am on my own at present.' (Which was true enough for Holmes was nowhere to be seen). The Inspector glanced around the sitting room casually, but I realised that he was taking more than a passing interest in all that he saw. 'Quite a smoker I see, Mr. Hargreaves. Pipes, tobacco and cigars in the coal scuttle. That has a familiar ring to it as has the Turkish slipper. I am myself a Holmesian, having always found Doyle's detective masterly. I see you have even gone to the trouble of obtaining an old sepia photograph of a diva and signed it 'Irene Adler'. Quite touching . . . no, no, please do not try to excuse an interest in which we share.' I was over defensive, 'Surely an interest in Sherlock Holmes does not make me into a suspect for your present investigation?' He looked at me shrewdly, 'Why, Mr. Hargreaves, who ever suggested that you were a suspect?' I didn't know what to say but he saved my embarrassment, 'However, as a professional crime writer you will know the next line?' I said, 'You mean the one where you say, 'Just don't leave town'?'

He laughed quite pleasantly, 'Something like that, but don't worry about it, Mr. Hargreaves, this is only routine stuff.'

When the policemen had gone, Holmes suddenly reappeared saying, 'I heard everything, Hargreaves. I was in the bedroom, and what I have heard makes me quite determined to try and prove your innocence. After all, if I do so it will save us all a great deal of embarrassment.'

The next surprise was exactly that and occurred on the very next day, preceded by a robust knocking at the front door. From the top of the stairs the silhouette of a head wearing a wide brimmed hat set against the glass panel showed me that my caller was a tall man indeed. I opened the door to reveal an enormous caped figure, and there in a cloud of cigar smoke, stood Orson Welles. Another man, scarcely much smaller of stature, stood in the background whilst across the road, poised as if for instant action, crouched a ferret faced man, waving an envelope.

'Greg, old man. Garrison gave me your

address. Quick, let us in and I'll explain, but whatever you do, don't admit yonder polecat!' I let them in and slammed the door against the advance of the ferrety one. Ignoring pleadings and threats delivered through the letterbox, I led my callers up the stairs and into the front room. Just to complicate everything, there in the bay of the front windows, stood Sherlock Holmes.

Welles started slightly at the sight of Holmes and then said, 'By George, Greg, for a second or two I thought you had got Basil staying with you!' Holmes introduced himself as Cyril Raymond.

Orson's companion proved to be one Holtz Wolfstein and was introduced as 'My colleague, fellow writer and co-conspirator'. Wolfstein had a strong face that lit up delightfully with a charming smile. Orson continued, 'Holtz is helping me to evade my tormentors, Greg. They have set that wretched weasel on me with his piece of paper.' I misunderstood, 'But with McCarthy's agent dead, I would have expected a lull in such activity.' Orson had not heard of the death and expressed his amazement when I explained. He took it in quickly saying, 'So Joe's errand boy has croaked his last? I'm not about to burst out crying, Greg, but in any case he was not bothering me. The little guy outside is a process server. They call them bailiffs over here I guess.'

Orson's ignorance concerning Craig's death was understandable because I knew him to be a man who often ignored radio, television and newspapers for weeks at a time when following a particular interest with that single minded fervour for which he was famous. The news of the outside world was simply to him a distraction at such a period of creativity. He continued (sounding rather like an erring school-boy), 'It seems I owe a little money, old man, not much, only a few thousand, and dollars at that, not pounds, but this pesky little guy is making normal life and business difficult. You see, I need to get to the St. James' Theatre within the hour, where I have to charm some moneymen into becoming backers. I want them to put up the dough, so that Holtz and I can put on a stage version of *Wuthering Heights*. It's going to be great old man. I play the actor manager reading the play to the cast. More like a one man show really without scenery. We can put it on for peanuts, but I can't risk showing up with the broker's man in tow . . . it's a serious production, not a pantomime!'

I suggested, 'You could accept the summons and be rid of him.' Orson shook his head, 'Worse, Greg. If I take the paper and cannot pay, I might be arrested, and that creates a really bad impression. Meanwhile I'm absolutely starving to death!' I hastily cooked what passes for sausages in Britain. A dozen, most of which Orson demolished, washing them down with my lukewarm beer. Holmes, practised in the art of refusing meals, sat at the table with us. Welles eyed him with interest, 'Cyril, you are perchance an actor?' Holmes replied, 'No, a retired investigator.' Orson chuckled, 'A gumshoe, eh? Well if you are retired that either means hiding from the mob or a health problem. Say, you do look a little peaky.' Sherlock shrugged, 'Maybe so, but my mind is still active enough for me to be able to suggest a solution to your present problem, albeit a temporary one. Your friend is near enough your own height, and sturdy enough of build to represent you should he don your outer garments. He could lead your tormentor a merry dance, leaving you to fulfil your engagement at the St. James' Theatre.'

Orson all but choked on a piece of sausage. After Holtz and I had banged him on the back, he turned to face Holmes with his vast beaming face, 'Cyril old buddy, you are a genius!' Holmes nodded and said, 'I believe that is a term that has often been used to describe us both.'

We quickly set to work to disguise Holtz with Orson's cape and stetson. When the brim was pulled well down and his slimmer neck hidden with a scarf, he passed muster we reckoned. Welles clapped his hands with glee, fairly shouting, 'Capital, leave here like that in a furtive manner and he'll follow you for sure. Lead him on as long as you can, Holtz. In fact, try to give me three hours and, in return, I promise to sell the backers on our enterprise.' As a finishing touch Holtz changed shoes with Orson, and their difference in foot size produced a limp that resembled that of Welles with his *gamé* leg. When Holtz lit an Orsonian corona, perfection was produced.

We watched from the window as Holtz, puffing cigar smoke like a caped locomotive, limped swiftly down Baker Street, with the seedy one loping in his wake. Orson shook the sitting room with his laughter, 'Gentlemen, I thank you with all my heart. Holtz's camel hair and beret are hardly my style but will suffice to get me to the theatre.' Once again Holmes and I had a royal box type view as Welles hailed a cab in the street below. Holmes grunted, 'He should have waited for the third cab. You do realise, Hargreaves, that your friend will be a suspect? His name appears upon that infamous sheet of paper.' He said this with an assertiveness that surprised me, 'How can you be sure of that, even if you have been to the scene of the crime. The police will surely have removed it?' Holmes said, 'Of course, but

I knew that they would have taken it to Scotland Yard and that is where I have been. It was, of course, filed and so unavailable to me, but fortunately the names of the suspects, your own included, had been chalked upon a blackboard.'

Amazed by his industry and touched by his efforts on my behalf after I had treated him so badly, I simply asked him, 'What other names were there?' He replied, 'An actor, Wayne Johnson, a Miss Winifred Shultz and an actress with a most unusual name, Miss Peppy Clovis. Do you know anything about these people?'

I thought carefully, before making a long and surprisingly, uninterrupted reply. 'Well yes, I know them all as it happens. Winni Shultz is a good little actress who works hard at finding and playing small parts and is about as communistic as Princess Elizabeth. Peppy Clovis is different. I worked with her last year making a commercial for 'Wondergleam' toothpaste. We chose her because she was bright and had good teeth, but I think on reflection, that she would do anything to further her career, and I do mean anything.'

He nodded and asked, 'How about Wayne Johnson?' I warned him that it was a long story. 'Wayne Johnson is an interesting guy. Some while back there was a very well known actor, James Hunter, who was fast becoming a big star. He was a young fellow with a brooding style that suited the mean and moody trend of a year or two back. Unfortunately he had earlier played parts for one of these left wing theatre groups, the very stuff that McCarthy's paranoia feeds on. He was one of the first to be named and destroyed, because he admitted his affiliations and refused to name names without apology. Here the story takes a tragic but interesting turn . . . '

I paused but Holmes made no sign that he wished me to stop talking, so I continued, 'James Hunter was blacklisted and such was McCarthy's influence that they even had to stop work on the picture that he had almost completed for the Kessler Brothers. Then came the tragedy.

James Hunter took his own life with an over the cliff plunge in his car.'

Holmes interrupted me at this point to ask, 'It was proven then that he took his own life without suspicion of foul play?' I replied, 'Well, his body was not recovered and had evidently been washed out to sea.' Holmes grew a little impatient, 'Please get to the point, Hargreaves. What has the story of Hunter's suicide to do with Wayne Johnson?' I tried to clarify the whole thing, cutting all the corners. 'With only a few scenes left to shoot the studio naturally wanted to finish the picture and cut their losses, so they searched for an actor who looked like Hunter, figuring that they could manage the last scenes that way if they avoided any close ups. They found an unknown young actor, Wayne Johnson, who looked a lot like him except that he had very little hair and a fairly recent scar on his left cheek. They tested him and found that with a suitable wig and heavy make up he could pass for Hunter well enough to settle their emergency. Ironically, he proved to be such a good actor that he got offers of other parts. His initial break had come through looking like Hunter, but subsequently he needed to look less like him, and so he specialised in character roles, usually bearded or with other dramatic changes to his appearance. Eventually he was getting roles that might once have been given to Hunter. He was as good an actor and had the advantage of not having attracted the attention of McCarthy, a great plus in Hollywood in recent times.'

Holmes looked thoughtful, 'Yet he was on Craig's list, and so, by the way, is Lyle Garrison.' I gasped, 'Garrison was chalked up on the wall as well? Wow, I can't imagine what for, because McCarthy has no business pestering a British national.' Holmes shrugged and said, 'He may have wanted Craig to try and extract information from him even if he had no legal right. After all, Garrison may be a fly in the McCarthy ointment simply through encouraging dubious American actors . . . and writers?' I did not like the inference of his last two words but I let it go.

5

At this point an interlude occurred which I did not particularly welcome. Hudson knocked at the door and asked if he might watch a programme on my television set. 'I don't have a television myself, Mr. Hargreaves, but I see from the paper that Tracey Comstock is being interviewed on *Cyclorama* and she is a particular favourite of mine. A lovely girl with a beautiful voice, don't you think?' I grunted assent and let him in, being sure that Holmes had heard his voice and could himself decide on his own next move. As it happened Holmes was absent from the sitting room when I ushered Hudson to a seat from which he could watch the tiny screen, which even way back then was becoming such a part of our lives.

I turned it on and after some kind of interlude signal, the captions for *Cyclorama* appeared. It was a quiet British version of what we would back home call a 'talk show'. There was a host, one George Gambling, a lean hawkeyed man, and as dry as a twig. He said, 'Hello viewers, welcome to *Cyclorama*, the programme where we try to keep you in touch.' He didn't say in touch with what, but then he was, for a television interviewer, a man of few words. Miss Comstock came on quite early in the show, answered a few questions about her new disc (Gambling referred to it as a gramophone record) and sung a few bars of it. I was hoping that once she had departed Hudson might do the same but he did not stir. Next there appeared a comedian with lines that seemed so unfunny to me that I suspected him of having a secret code just for his fans. A left wing politician came on and ranted, but Gambling gave him a hard time, and still Hudson sat as if turned to stone. The final guest was a pleasing surprise to me for it was Orson Welles, talking about his production of what I had mentally dubbed 'Wuthering without the Heights'. Evidently Hudson had seen enough and hastily took his leave, interrupting the only part of the programme that held any interest for me. He said, 'You'll excuse me, Mr. Hargreaves, but I have to attend a meeting of my musical society . . . thanks for letting me see Miss Comstock!'

I tried to concentrate on the remainder of Orson's interview. I could tell that he just wanted to talk about his forthcoming production, but Gambling had other ideas and kept goading him concerning past work. 'Is it true that Senator Joseph McCarthy is claiming that your so called masterpiece, *Citizen Kane*, is communistic?' Welles all but exploded. He had been in the act of lighting one of his eternal cigars but was so outraged that he forgot about it and allowed the still lit match to burn his fingers. He shook his fingers angrily and fixed Gambling with huge dilated eyes saying, 'I don't know, but he can claim anything he likes. Just let him invite me to give evidence at one of his so called hearings, if he dares!'

'McCarthy would be well advised to avoid such a step I think!' I suddenly realised that these words emanated not from Gambling but from Sherlock Holmes who had suddenly reappeared. He let me watch and listen to the rest of Orson's interview in peace. Gambling might have been as dull as ditch water, but he was skilled in debate and niggled away at Welles in order to try and make him seem like a communist. He enquired, 'What then is your political philosophy?' Orson rapped out his brilliant reply, 'I am not interested in politics so I have no such philosophy, but I have beliefs and one of them is that the ordinary decent people of this world be granted freedom of thought, deed and speech so that they can continue their lawful pursuits . . . (he paused thoughtfully, at last lighting the neglected cigar) . . . such as going to the theatre to see me in *Wuthering Heights*!' Then he burst into infectious Wellesian laughter as the captions rolled.

'So your friend has got the wherewithal to enable him to put on his theatrical performance, Hargreaves? More power to him. His handling of Gambling makes one understand why he has a reputation for upsetting the establishment. Oh, and, by the by, friend Hudson spoke the truth about his affiliation to a musical group. I have frequently seen him enter the local hall where the meetings of Orchestral International are held.'

Holmes spent the rest of the afternoon and part of the evening with me, but whilst the Craig mystery occupied much of our conversation, there were intervals of a purely social nature. For example, we started a game of chess, prompted by my discovery of a board and pieces in one of the sideboard drawers. Of course, I was required to make all of the moves, but I soon realised that I stood little chance of beating the most brilliant mind in Great Britain, if not the world. However, those long intervals between the actual movements of the pieces let me play for time and attempt to distract him with my frequent questions. Eventually I asked him what, back home, would be called the sixty-four thousand dollar question. 'Holmes, we have had a little time to think about it and we know who the suspects are . . . Orson, Garrison, Johnson, Winni and Peppy. Oh, and I nearly forgot to include myself. Based then on what we already know, who do you think is guilty of killing Craig?' He said, 'White bishop takes pawn. Who do I think killed Craig? I never answer a question like that with an 'I think', Hargreaves, for the answer to such a question would need to be preceded by the words 'I know'. I am greatly handicapped by my present situation which makes a complete investigation by myself impossible. I can only work with my head, rather as a rugby player with both hands tied behind him. I need more facts my dear fellow, and to find them I must for the first time in my life rely to some extent upon the physical efforts of others, mainly yourself.'

He indicated an alarmed frustration with his own handicaps. I felt so sorry for this brilliant man who had always been so independent. A man doomed to be unable to play chess unless his opponent made his moves for him, although I knew that in him hung my real chance of being released from all suspicion in the Craig affair. My troubled friend did, however, allow himself some observations on the subject that so preoccupied me. 'As for yourself, well we know, Hargeaves, that you are innocent even if we are unable to prove it, and I am reasonably sure that your friend Welles is quite blameless.'

I enquired, 'Do you have reason to say that, other than intuition?' 'Why yes, Hargreaves, I have visited the scene of the crime. The victim's desk was centred on a deep pile carpet, and careful inspection of it revealed indentations recently made by shoes or boots.' I butted in, 'But would the police not have been trampling on it?' He chuckled, 'Reynolds is not brilliant, but he has at least an average degree of intellect. Even Lestrade would have prevented such a disturbance. No, it was easy to see which marks were made by the assailant, and they were not made by friend Welles.' 'How can you be so sure?' Holmes said, 'He is an extremely large man with feet in proportion to his size. There were no traces of size twelves!' I asked, 'Might he not have squeezed his feet into smaller shoes just to leave a misleading trail?' Sherlock shook his head sadly at my lack of experience, 'Do you think a man of his weight, twenty stone if an ounce, could have disguised the depth of the impressions made by his feet? No, Hargreaves, I do not believe your friend to be involved.' I brightened, 'That leaves only four suspects, Wayne, Winni, Peppy, and of course, Lyle Garrison.' He nodded, 'Four official suspects. Let us then consider them. Do you really mean to leave your knight unguarded? Wayne Johnson appears, on the surface, to have benefited rather than suffered at the hands of the witch hunter. Lyle Garrison has seen the terrible results of the witch hunt and may well be more than sympathetic towards the victims of McCarthy. You have evidence of his attitude. He's mild mannered and in a position of some influence . . . not a very likely candidate. Stranger things have happened though, Hargreaves. Thank goodness you castled, because I don't want the game to end quite so quickly. We know rather less about the two women. The girl with the silly name, Peppy. You have told me little of her save that she appeared in a toothpaste advertisement. Oh yes, and what of Winifrid Shultz, you have told me next to nothing about her save that she is a good actress. I suggest that we should concentrate our efforts on the female suspects for a while.'

I agreed but enquired, 'When I said that there were four suspects you corrected me with the addition of the word 'official'. What did you mean by this?' He said, 'Experience has shown me, Hargreaves, that the guilty party in such a case is quite often someone outside of the official ring of suspects. However, until we can cast our net more widely, we must investigate nearer to home. I suggest that you make a start by inviting one of the two ladies to come and see you. Would Miss Shultz accept an invitation from you for a quiet meal and a chat?'

Winifred's phone number I obtained from Lyle Garrison. I called her and invited her over for the following evening. We colluded, Holmes and I, so that he could hear all my questions and her answers by the courtesy of the Grundig Company. It was Holmes' idea, which showed just how quickly he could accept an innovation, once he was aware of it. He said, 'If I hide in the bedroom I may not be able to hear everything, and she may not take to me in person (remember your experience with the blonde lady). How long does the tape run?' I said, 'About an hour.' He rejoined, 'That should be long enough if you are well rehearsed and switch it on at just the right time.' I hid the machine behind a small inverted screen on the sideboard and placed a bowl of flowers in front of it. 'I can switch it on under cover of moving the bowl.'

Winifred seemed quite delighted with the idea of accepting an invitation for a meal and a chat, especially as I had baited my invitation with the tiny hint of a possible part for her in the 'Walton' television series. She was no more than ten minutes late. I decided to get all the small talk over with before switching on the Grundig. I took her coat and laid it on my bed, returning to the sitting room to pour her a drink. I had taken the trouble to purchase a selection of liqueurs but she would accept only wine, and white wine at that. My culinary experiment was sizzling away in the oven, thanks to Philip Harben's television programme.

'So, Greg, tell me all about yourself and what you have been doing. I was so sorry to hear about your brush with his satanic majesty, but I hear you've struck oil over here!' I was non-committal, 'Yes, and no. I've sold Garrison on being more than a little bit interested in my angling detective, Walton.' She wrinkled her nose, 'Yuk, angling! That means putting slimey things on hooks, darling. I can't see a future for little old me there!' I was surprised at how such a good and well established actress could be so foolishly dismissive before knowing fully what might be in store for her, but then I realised that it was part of a 'little girl' act that she was putting on for my benefit. I said, 'Don't dismiss my project out of hand, honey, you might find the details more interesting. Orson might be playing the laird, and they haven't cast his lady yet.'

114

She squawked with false joy, 'Darling, how lovely, I'm good at the aristocracy. Did you see me in *Lady Windermere's Fan*? I played Lady Windermere's friend!' I excused myself and went off to the kitchen to see to Harben's 'quiche', and then having dished it up I brought in the plates and put them on the dining table. I had set it out in a fairly spartan manner, so the movement of the bowl of flowers to make a centrepiece seemed natural, and the Grundig was all but silent. I started to pump her for information about herself, making it as casual as I could, 'Orson was here a few days back. Do you know him?' She giggled in a refined manner, 'Orson? I should say so! Why during the late stages of the war, when I was little more than a 'bobbysoxer', he sawed me in half! It was one of those times when Rita was throwing fits, and Delores was old news, whilst Marlene was out of the country.' I remembered Orson's *Mercury Wonder Show* that he had presented under canvas for 1,150 performances. I had even donned a fez and trundled on some piece of equipment for Welles just to make up

115

the numbers on one occasion.

I recalled thinking at the time that Orson should have been a professional illusionist. It would have deprived the world of *Citizen Kane*, *The Magnificent Ambersons* and other masterpieces, but Orson himself would have kept his dangerous weight problem in control through constant work and touring, with his own theatrical production to salve his artistic conscience. I asked, 'Were you ever in any of his off-Broadway productions?' She replied, 'No, Greg, I had more sense than to get into that left wing trap. I saw the writing on the wall a long time ago. Isn't it awful about Lionel Craig. I knew him very well you know. In fact it was he who first warned me about the un-American business a few years back. We had a thing going you know, but he started to smother me with his attentions and so I decided to get out of the affair. It wasn't that easy because he was a very forceful guy, and I suppose his pride was hurt.' I asked, 'He gave you a hard time?' She replied, 'Yes, he kept showing up at my place at all the wrong times, to the extent that I had to call in the cops. Speaking of whom, the English variety got in touch with me over Craig's death. Goodness knows where they got my name and address from.' I said, 'Well, I don't imagine you could have been much help to them.' She said, 'You are darn right. Haven't seen him in years, I'm happy to say.'

She tired of small talk, and wanted to get down to business, 'So you think you could interest Lyle in offering me a part in your fishing epic, Greg? I know it's only television, but that little old contraption is the future for us all, isn't it?' She nodded her blonde head in the general direction of my HMV, her remarks telling me that she was shrewder and deeper than she seemed. I said, 'I can't make any promises, as I have already indicated, but Lyle knows your work and I feel sure that he would be interested to know that you were available. He's bought an option and a couple of days ago he gave me the go ahead to work on the scripts.' Then with half a tape left to record I tried a more daring ploy, telling Winni a very heavily censored version of my own useless alibi concerning Craig's death. Needless to say, I left out all mention of Sherlock Holmes, the 'Baker Street Ghost'! She raised her eyebrows and said, 'Naughty, naughty, Greg . . . and what a pity you can't trace this trollop!' I played a card tentatively, 'At least I'm never likely to forget where I was on that particular evening.' She said, 'Me too, I was having dinner with Rex and Kay. He's a pain but she is sweet . . . I phoned them the following day to thank them and it was Kay who gave me the news. She has a fearsome little pug dog you know. Fortunately it is very old and quite toothless, but it can gum one nearly to death!' She had turned the talk to trivia, but I could read from her face that she half suspected that I was fishing for information concerning her movements. However, I wisely left the subject and did not mention Craig again. Instead I made small movie and show business talk. By the time she left in a cab around midnight, I believe she had all but forgotten my minor blunder.

The following day I ran the tape for Holmes, who sat silently through it, small talk, plates rattling, glass clinking and all. He sat listening impassively with his long slim fingers tip to tip in a characteristic attitude. When the Grundig whirred to signify that the end had come, I switched it off and gave him all my attention saying, 'Not a lot of use, I fear, for it just seems to prove her blameless.' Holmes raised an eyebrow at me, 'My dear Hargreaves, just because Miss Shultz has a cast iron alibi is no proof that she has no connection with the crime. Let us consider it all. She knew the murder victim well. Well enough indeed to have had with him an *affaire d'amour*, and causing him to become a nuisance to her. According to her she had nothing to fear from him in his official capacity, but he was an influential man and such men are often dangerous to those with whom they have some grudge. Remember also, that a person does not always need to be present at the actual criminal act to be guilty of it, at least, in part.' I asked, 'You mean she might have hired someone else to kill him?' He said, 'Yes, and it would be interesting to know if her dinner engagement came to her out of the blue at short notice, or if it was brought about at her own suggestion. These people, Rex and Kay, you appear to know them. Are they respectable, responsible and beyond reproach?' I said, 'Rex Harrison and Kay Kendal are both very well established in the theatre. In fact, I think one could say that they were part of the establishment, almost as much as Larry and Vivienne.' Holmes nodded, for he knew who Larry and Vivienne were. 'Well, she seems an unlikely suspect, Hargreaves, but we cannot rule her out altogether. I wish I could have been there to lead her with questions but, nevertheless, you did well.'

I had aired the sitting room in order to prepare it for the visit of Winifred Shultz, but now Holmes insisted that I close the windows and refill it with the 'Scottish Mixture' fumes. I did this, working so relentlessly with the clay pipe, that I began to fear for my throat, my lungs and indeed my health in general. But Sherlock would hear nothing of my fears for my constitution, saying, 'Tobacco is a stimulant to the brain, but it is also a disinfectant. In addition flies, midges and other small tiresome insects hate it!' I told him that I had seen a piece in *The Times* by an eminent physician, linking smoking with lung cancer. He laughed, 'My dear Hargreaves, I smoked a huge amount of tobacco during more than fifty years of my life, in addition to punishing my system with intermittent periods of cocaine use. I also smoked cigars and cigarettes, both Virginian and Egyptian. I lived into my seventies, Hargreaves, and through that long life I have known far more old smokers than old doctors.'

6

A day or so later, I had another visit from Inspector Reynolds, that occurred whilst I was working on 'Walton'. Holmes was fortunately walking in the zoo at the time. (Or such had been his expressed intention). Reynolds was almost jovial, 'Thought you'd be pleased to hear that we have made an arrest in connection with the Craig murder inquiry.' I craftily crossed to the sideboard and turned on the Grundig that was still set behind the three-fold screen. I did this under the pretext of producing glasses to offer the Inspector a drink. He allowed me to pour him some of that warm beer that would have made me a notorious host in California. He accepted saying, 'I'm not on duty and, in any case, I have never really considered you as a suspect. No, I always had a sneaking suspicion regarding the man we have arrested, Mr. Lyle Garrison!'

122

For me, it was as if I were in the London of the previous decade with a bomb dropping. I could not believe that Garrison was even suspected let alone arrested. I almost stammered, 'But whatever has given you grounds to suspect him?' He smiled, 'We move at our own speed, slow but sure. A thorough investigation at the scene of the crime turned up a threatening letter written to Craig from Garrison. Oh, and by the way (he dropped his second bombshell) you were the subject of the disagreement.' I gasped, 'I was?' 'Yes it seems that Garrison had received a note, or a phone call, from Craig suggesting that he should not employ you if he did not want any trouble with American distributors. The letter which we have at Scotland Yard is from Garrison, advising Craig that should he continue to poke his nose into British cinematographic affairs it would be the worst for him. What do you think about that?' I was appalled. 'Can I see the letter?' He dropped his smile, 'No fear, it's at the Yard as I have said. It is evidence and under wraps at present.' I then asked the obvious, 'Is there anything I can do to help Mr. Garrison?' He looked at me with a sphinx-like expression, 'Only if you know more of this affair than you have told me, and I don't really think you do.' I agreed, 'I don't. Tell me, as I know little of the British legal system; will he get bail?' He nodded, 'Oh yes, I imagine so, once a charge has been made. With a man in his position it is usual.' I couldn't think of much more to say except, 'You know people in our business use very dramatic terms. If Garrison said it would be the worst for Craig, he probably just meant that he would put the matter into the hands of his solicitor.' He nodded dubiously, 'Yes, well others more important than I will decide about that. Anyway, I must be on my way, and of course I will want to speak with you again. You may be required to give evidence.' As he prepared to leave, Reynolds turned and said with a hint of irony, 'By the way, Mr. Hargreaves, it may be an easy matter to hide a tape recorder from view, but it is extremely difficult to eliminate that slight unmistakable hiss that it makes. We have one at the Yard. A very useful instrument, but a pity that such recordings do not count as evidence in court.'

When Holmes returned from his walk as suddenly as he had left for it, I told him of the Inspector's visit and the bombshell that he had delivered. He was surprised but not as amazed as I had been. I played the tape for him and he laughed at the Inspector's final words. 'Upon my word, Hargreaves, we have slightly underestimated Reynolds. I doubt that Lestrade would have noticed the hiss of the recorder, even had they existed in his day. Mind you, he was slightly deaf in his left ear. I deduced this from the way he stood when addressed, and the habit he had of placing one palm on the side of his head when concentrating upon a sound. By the way, the trees are splendid in the park, and the sea lions are in excellent condition.'

We tried to return to our chess game, but I could not concentrate, with the result that Holmes declared, 'Check-mate!' and I was forced to knock my king over. I said, 'I have to help Lyle Garrison, Holmes, for several reasons. He is a swell guy. He is presently essential to my career, and he didn't do it!' Holmes shook a bony finger at me and said, 'Ah, Hargreaves, your first two points may be so, but the third and final point is pure conjecture on your part. We do not yet know who killed Craig and the introduction of this letter has to point to at least a possibility of Garrison's guilt.' I said warmly, 'But you do not think that he did it?' He admonished me again, 'You know my answer to that!' I nodded sadly, 'You never merely think, but can only deduce, examine all facts and never discard any possibility whilst it remains so. I know your methods, Holmes, but I implore you to help me to clear Garrison.' He said, 'I will assist you to find the guilty person in this matter, be it Garrison, one of the other suspects, or a person as yet unknown.'

We decided between us that we knew quite a lot about Garrison, Johnson and Winni Shultz. This left Peppy Clovis. I knew her a little better than I cared to admit to Holmes, but aside from that which I had already told him, I knew little more that could have been helpful. We decided, therefore, that I should hold another dinner party, but in order that Peppy should not get the wrong idea, Holmes would be present as well, making Grundig's invitation unnecessary! We would, we decided, pass Sherlock off as a long lost relative of mine, recuperating from a nasty illness to excuse his crimson robe. I knew Peppy would jump at my invitation once I told her of my great expectations regarding television.

I was right, of course, and Peppy managed to work me into a rather complicated web of social engagements. 'Greg, darling, is this the brilliant friend you promised to introduce me to?' She smiled bewitchingly at Holmes, who bowed his head and indicated a chair for her to sit in. Peppy had always struck me as being a sort of reincarnation of a character from the roaring twenties, with her beaded purse and long cigarette holder. Sometimes I had half expected her to be wearing a *cloche* hat over her neatly parcelled blonde hair. She was rather like Jean Harlow though rather more animated facially. I opened the champagne and she poured some gratefully into her small, but beautifully formed, mouth.

She glanced at Holmes again and said, 'You know, Cyril, (we had again used the Cyril Raymond alias) your health problem may emanate from your mind rather than that old body. I have a friend, a good friend, a psychologist, Professor John Wardle. I was a real mess mentally, darling, but he sorted me out and even introduced me to some influential people who furthered my career. I'll leave you his phone number before I go.' Holmes thanked her politely and said, 'My mind is certainly more likely to respond to treatment than my body, and I am always anxious to meet persons of influence.' I had always suspected that a fine sense of humour lurked beneath his clinical exterior and he seemed to be offering me proof of this now. We talked movie trivialities for a while, but as we started on the *pâté* I had obtained from Harrods and the champagne started to take effect, Peppy became more and more talkative. At first she spent a lot of time trying to get Holmes to eat, which was, of course, impossible. I had to explain to her that he was being nourished through a daily medical infusion and was forbidden other food or drink. He bolstered this statement of mine by saying, 'Dear lady, do not concern yourself for my well being. I have received all the nourishment that I presently need.' This was, of course, perfectly true and at length she desisted in her attempts to temp his appetite. 'I knew a guy once, an old guy, who could only eat or drink through a tube in his side. One day I visited him and there was a tea tray next to his bed. He invited me to pour myself some. That I did. Then I asked him if he would care to take some tea. He nodded and I poured him a cup, but he reminded me saying, 'pour it down the tube'. I did so and he jumped about a foot in the air. I was worried and asked, 'Gee, was it too hot?' He said, 'No, you forgot to put the sugar in!' Well, I laughed, I can tell you. Cyril, darling, how long will you need to keep off the solids and liquids. It must be awful?' Holmes said vaguely, 'Oh quite some time.'

By the time she had picked at my attempt at beef goulash, downed several more glasses of champagne and was seated in an armchair nursing a glass of brandy, Peppy Clovis was fairly talking her head off. 'You know this McCarthy business is just about the limit isn't it? I tell you, if it weren't for a few brave souls like yourself, Greg, he would be doing exactly what he wanted with the movie business. I guess he wants to control it for some purpose of his own. How fortunate that Lyle is standing up against him, at least as far as this country is concerned. Craig's death may be unfortunate but perhaps it will give you guys a break?' I told her of Garrison's arrest and she almost dropped her brandy glass. 'Lyle arrested? But he didn't do it. He's not that sort of guy. Is this going to ruin your television series and my chance to get a part in it?' I reassured her to some extent but I could see that she was shaken enough to have dropped her act, seeming to be a little more concerned than I might have expected her to be. Holmes was watching and listening with rapt attention as she prattled on, 'This has ruined everything. You wait until John hears about this ... ' I assumed that she referred to the Professor Wardle whom she had mentioned earlier, but she seemed to realise that she had said too much and became defensive. 'I mean John Robins, a guy I know who is very interested in the McCarthy business. Of course, it doesn't concern me personally except where it spoils my chances to advance my career ... ' She tailed off and I refilled her brandy glass. She brightened, realising that she had been unwise and started to prattle again in her earlier bright fashion.

She turned to Holmes, 'I expect you find this shop talk boring Cyril darling, not being in the business yourself. Tell me, what is your particular line of business?' Holmes told her that he was a retired apiarist, though he had to explain what an apiarist was. She seemed intrigued, unless it was part of her act.

'Gosh! Cyril, who would have thought that you kept bees. I guess it is all that honey that makes you such a sweetie!'

At this point Holmes decided to produce his own strange version of turning on the charm. He held us both on the edges of our chairs with stories concerning hives and queens, drones and worker bees. An unlikely subject with which to attempt to enthral a young woman, but then he was a master with words when he needed to be. I had seen this hinted at by scribe Watson, but had not realised just how much personal magnetism was involved. Peppy seemed to forget all her guarded subjects as she said, 'Greg, your friend is a real charmer, you should try and work him into your television series, assuming that Lyle gets out of his trouble . . . ' Mention of Lyle Garrison's arrest brought just a shadow of her defensive manner back, but Holmes charmed that away by saying, 'Dear lady, you are too kind, but I fear that my histrionics have been confined to some college theatricals in my youth, but please will you remember to give me the telephone number of your Professor Wardle. If he can help me, who knows, the next time we meet I might be in better shape.' She scribbled a number on the back of her visiting card and handed it to him, smiling bewitchingly. I luckily managed to nudge her elbow so that she dropped the card. I picked it up and layed it upon the arm of Holmes' chair.

After Peppy had departed, I asked Holmes to give me his reaction to the events and conversations of my little dinner party. He smiled, 'You showed great presence of mind, Hargreaves, in handling that situation concerning the card with the telephone number. At last we begin to work like a team. This Professor Wardle interests me. He may have absolutely no involvement with matters that concern us, but there was something in her words concerning him that pointed to something unusual. A psychologist who not only heals through the mind, but makes introductions of a darkly hinted influential nature. You must phone him, Hargreaves, and arrange an appointment for me.'

I did just that, being amazed to find that I was able to arrange for Holmes to see Wardle on the very next day, with Peppy's name seeming to work the oracle. Whilst at the phone box I dialled Garrison's number and was delighted to hear him answer in person. 'Greg, I've had a little trouble, some misunderstanding with the police but I am sure it will sort itself out. I want you to come over and have a script conference. I'm planning to start shooting 'Walton', or rather its first episode, very shortly.'

I explained to Holmes that I would be talking with Lyle Garrison at about the same time as he would be consulting Wardle. He said, 'Excellent, Watson . . . that is Hargreaves . . . we are a team indeed. Find out what you can from Garrison, short of making him suspect interrogation, and I shall do the same with the professor. Evidently your friend, Miss Clovis, has influence with him or is it *vice versa?* Tomorrow night we will exchange experiences.' He disappeared but he didn't throw me this time as I was getting used to his ways.

At the appointed time I had the 'Scottish Mixture' ready so that I could waft it's comforting fumes toward the 'Ghost of Baker Street'. 'Hargreaves, I would like your account of your meeting with Lyle Garrison.' I said, 'It's a longish story but I'll cut all the corners. I was there at his invitation to discuss 'Walton', which we did for most of the time. By the way they start filming it for television in just two weeks time. The speed with which they are tackling it, shows how hard up they are for a new series for the square-eyed monster! Now in America they . . . ' Holmes cut in testily, 'Yes, yes, Hargreaves, but you did say you were going to emulate Ducrow. I am not familiar with the expression you used concerning the corners, but I assume you meant to get to the point?' I sighed and recommenced my oration, 'We did discuss his arrest and the Craig affair. Naturally he proclaimed his innocence with such impassioned words that might have been believed by even the most cynical of listeners.'

Holmes gratefully breathed in the

tobacco fumes, 'I have listened to such statements too often and then proved the pleader to be guilty beyond doubt. Give me facts, Hargreaves, with which to work.' I explained, 'Well, he said he went for a walk on the Embankment and would have been there at the estimated time of the crime. He did not meet or converse with anyone he knew, or who could be likely to be traced. However, he didn't seem to me to be particularly concerned about the outcome of it all, saying that Craig had almost as many enemies as has the Senator from Wisconsin himself. When I suggested that his letter to Craig could have been misconstrued, he denied writing to Craig at all!' This interested Holmes, who said, 'I must try in some way to get a sighting of it. The Inspector must believe it to be genuine?' I replied, 'It was typed on his company's letterhead and signed with what certainly appeared to be his usual signature. He is not exactly in tears over Craig's demise, which must count against him.' Holmes said, 'Yes, but it is the letterhead and signature which really count against him.

Proof that they were forgeries could well clear him, but, Hargreaves, unless you have more momentous facts for me I will give some account of my meeting with Professor Wardle.'

I agreed and tried not to interrupt his narration, except where I thought that he might want me to. 'Wardle proved to be a man in his forties, of distinguished appearance and plausible manner. He was entirely undismayed by my bizarre appearance, having doubtless dealt with a great many eccentrics in his time.' I asked, 'Do you mean to say that you consider many of those who consult an analyst to be eccentric?' He grunted, 'Undoubtedly, Hargreaves, most of them pay the psychologist to tell them exactly that which they wish to hear, or else they are genuinely amazed when having answered a few questions the professor reveals facts about themselves which they feel he could not possibly know. In fact he listens, observes and then sells them back the information that they have given him. Fortune tellers work in much the same manner, but claim psychic powers. For example, he said to me, 'You know, sir, leaning upon narcotics and even stronger substances will not solve your problem, which I imagine is connected with your spending far too much time isolated from your fellow beings'. You see, Hargreaves, the ash upon my robe has grown no less distinguished since my demise. Also the tear in the left sleeve tends to reveal several interesting needle scars. One addicted to tobacco and various more serious narcotics is hardly likely to be the life and soul of the party, especially when given the greyness of my present complexion! He is shrewd, but quite without genuine qualifications. I managed to study the framed certificates upon his wall and all were from spurious trans-Atlantic sources unknown to me.'

I felt forced to ask, 'Could he not have other quite genuine qualifications?' He laughed mockingly, 'Upon my word, Hargreaves, that's a real 'Watsonian' remark. Can you imagine a man with real degrees in psychology displaying a certificate obtained from the 'North East Arkansas Society of Psychostudy'? Rather like Lord Rothschild attempting to pass a five pound note that he knew to be a forgery. No, the man is a fraud, but a quite convincing one. By the way, it will cost you ten guineas, Hargreaves. The bill will arrive here addressed to me in my latest persona, and you will, of course, pay it. I mentioned Miss Clovis by the way and this seemed to at least partially open a door. His whole manner changed and he started trying to decide if I was a bearer of information, or a seeker after feminine company.' I could not help but make an explosive enquiry at this point, 'Holmes, you are not serious?' He chuckled, 'Oh, yes, your lady friend is either a refined tout for an introduction agent, or someone on the fringe of some kind of espionage, or possibly both. He looked at me very strangely and asked, 'Are the crocuses doing well?' Obviously this was some sort of introduction to a password or coded reply. He recovered quickly when I merely shrugged and said 'Just something I ask my patients. You would be surprised at the reactions I get from a seemingly unconnected remark'.

Then having discovered that I was not the bearer of some secret information, he started to show me photographs of his female clients. Some of these portraits depicted the sitters in a minimum of clothing and his inferences would not even have escaped Lestrade! When I did not respond in a suitable manner, he brought the consultation to a close, suggesting that I think about what had been said and contact him again.'

Holmes reminded me to work harder on the 'Scottish Mixture' and after a short reverie, he said, 'Wardle, of course, may have nothing to do with the Craig affair, and Miss Clovis may be the only connecting, and possibly quite innocent, link, but what I have learned just might have some bearing on it all. However, let us reconsider your conversation with Garrison. Whilst I have been telling you about my consultation with Wardle, I have been turning over the matter of the letter which he claims not to have sent to Craig.' (During our short relationship, Holmes had several times sprung this extraordinary trait of his upon me. He seemed to be working at times on what the fly-boys during the war would have called an automatic pilot!) He continued, 'You have examples on file of letters signed and sent to you by Garrison, have you not?' I produced several letters from the only file I had, a sixpenny folder from Woolworths. I spread the letters that he might see them. He would like to have studied them through his lens but settled for my acting as an intermediary by holding my reading spectacles an inch or two above the pages. He grunted and said, 'He has a distinctive signature. Do you have any other examples of his writing?'

I produced the contract for 'Walton' which he also studied. Then he said, 'I notice that he always signs his name with a rather unusual purple ink. He signs his letters and contracts with an Onoto fountain pen of a fairly well established type. You will notice how the ink wells out in a very distinctive manner on the first letter in each example, a characteristic of the make. Just before my demise, Hargreaves, fountain pens were becoming popular enough for me to have made a study of them prior to writing a monograph upon them, which unfortunately I was not given the time to complete. Now let us consider the letterhead once more. Again identical in each case except for the contract. This is printed upon sheets of what appears to be the same headed notepaper at a glance, but warrants further study. It is not die sunk or indeed printed at all in the accepted style. Turn the sheets, Hargreaves, and you will, I'll wager, find no raised impressions at all. No, the document, is produced by means of a process unfamiliar to me. Hold it up that I may apply the nose test.' I held up a sheet from the contract, which he sniffed at in a truly inquisitive manner saying, 'Bromide, hypo and similar photographic chemicals. Could the existing letterhead have been copied photographically, Hargreaves?' I explained to him that I had heard about, though not encountered, a new process in which a copy could be made upon thin sensitised paper by placing the original and the sensitised paper face to face and then inserting them into a special machine. A hypo spray could then fix the resulting copy, made by the lighting of a bright electric bulb. He nodded, 'Photographic copying of documents, a natural progression from the making of blueprints has long existed, but was always a long and complicated process involving a copying camera and the printing out upon heavy bromide paper. In other words, the result could never have pretended to be anything but a copy, whilst what we have here could pass as an original to a casual observer.' I was amazed at how quickly even his astute mind took on board innovations so long after his time. He may have ceased to live, and may have been deprived of participation in life around him, but he had not been prevented from observing it!

7

The filming of 'Walton' had been in progress for quite some time with Lyle Garrison mercifully spared imprisonment to supervise it. I was invited to attend, which I did, though not on a regular basis, and even then keeping my involvement to an absolute minimum. I had, in the past, observed over anxious writers who interfered with filming, and had seen what eventually happened to them. I was happy to be working and getting paid for it and had no desire whatever to rock the boat, but when Holmes suddenly appeared among those upon the sidelines, I was a trifle worried. No pass had been issued to him, but then, nothing could stop him being wherever he wished. I explained away his presence to Lyle, who was entirely unworried by the appearance of an amiable eccentric in a worn red dressing robe.

I said, 'Lyle, I was on the point of

getting a pass for Cyril when he seemed to go missing, only to turn up here in the studio. Goodness knows how he managed to get in.' Garrison said kindly, 'Don't give it another thought, I've already got real problems to worry about as you know, but tell me, does he usually go around in his dressing gown?' I forced a chuckle and said, 'He's British, and you have more eccentrics to the square foot than I thought possible.' Lyle laughed despite his troubles and said, 'You have your fair share in Hollywood. I was once told that Valentino used to sleep in a glass coffin. Or was it Navarro?'

I had been a little fortunate in my ability to keep rash promises because Orson had returned to Baker Street to tell me of the premature closing of *Wuthering Heights*, brought about mainly through a breach in his friendship with Wolfstein. He had apparently turned out to be a martinet of an old man, once he had got his hands on the backing money that I had worked and slaved to get him. I sympathised, secretly rubbing my hands with glee, knowing that Garrison was ready to snap him up for a one episode *rôle* in 'Walton' as a kilted laird in the first story. Moreover, I had no difficulty in getting him to give Peppy Clovis a small part, so complete was his satisfaction concerning the 'gift' of Orson.

Thus I had kept all my promises and my world seemed to be quite serene. As Garrison sat in 'producer's corner' with his papers and clip boards, the director strode around and issued his orders to camera crew and actors. He was an intense young man with a British public school accent, Charterhouse possibly, for it had not the dominance of Eton or Harrow according to Holmes, who knew more about dialects than anyone I ever met, making Professor Higgins seem like an amateur.

I was soon to get an example of that which was Welles' strength and weakness all in one. In any scene in which he was involved the director was soon made redundant. He was, of course, quite magnificent in his *rôle*, and his suggestions to the cameraman and lighting crew were very sound. Every so often he would

146

call a sort of huddle in which I was forced, as writer, to take part. 'Greg old man, could you change this line so that I can get more majesty from it?' I was happy to comply, yet had to watch Lyle and the director carefully to be sure that I was not aiding and abetting in what might have seemed to have been a conspiracy of some kind. All went calmly enough until Welles dropped his bombshell in suggesting a really major change in the whole concept. He said, 'I believe the whole thing would be more interesting and entertaining if you were to cast a woman as Walton!'

I had often wondered at the British expression concerning the introduction of a feline amongst the avian species, but now I had a perfect example of a cat being placed among the pigeons. There was much ranting, raving, pleading and moaning, but in the end the director walked off the set in a huff. Garrison, who could see the strength of Orson's suggestion, was happy to do the recasting and a certain amount of re-shooting, which this would involve, but was stuck with the fact that he had to find another director at extremely short notice. He turned to me, the least influential of his circle and pleaded, 'What am I going to do, Greg. If I don't find a director almost at once we will go way over budget and my first television series might be my ruination . . . even before I am hung for the murder of McCarthy's toad!' I felt so sorry, especially as I seemed indirectly responsible. I found myself daring to say, 'You could ask Orson to direct?'

There was an electric silence, broken by Garrison turning to Welles and asking, 'Orson, you wouldn't direct the series for me would you?' The big fellows reaction was immediate and, for me, predictable. 'Lyle old man, how can I refuse, having, without meaning to, caused you some problems. I made what I thought was a good suggestion which would lift your series out of the rut it was ploughing for itself, and the snooty guy just took off. Let us finish today's scenes where Walton does not appear and tomorrow we can start to re-shoot as many scenes as we must. I'm sure Greg will do the small amount of rewriting required?' I nodded asking, 'But who is to play Miss Walton?'

A hasty conference promoted Peppy Clovis to the starring *rôle*. Orson said he knew her work and that he thought that she could do it. Garrison was a little more worried concerning the promotion of a small part player in such lightning style, but having listened to Peppy reading a line or two agreed that she should be tried at least. Crazy as it all sounds, Peppy was aged twenty years in make up and proved to be brilliant as Miss Walton. As for her progress since, well it is cinematographic history. Meanwhile, I mused that the cast was a strong one anyway, including Orson, Winni Shultz and Wayne Johnson, made up to look as little like Hunter as possible. Orson and Peppy left together, Welles having promised to coach her in her *rôle*. I walked out of the studio accompanied by Holmes and Johnson. Along the exit corridor we passed a row of those huge star portraits that were still popular in the fifties. There they were, already a dated gallery that included Nelson Eddy, Jack Buchanan,

Gracie Fields and John Hunter. As we reached Hunter's portrait, Wayne postured in front of it, striking a similar affected pose to the depicted actor he so closely resembled. He said, 'Poor old Hunter, mined by McCarthy, but took a sensible way out. When he did away with himself, he lost me my job as his double, but thanks to character make ups I may turn a tragedy into advantage. After all, it's better to be an actor than a ghost!'

Back at Hudson House, Holmes and I discussed the events of the day. He said, 'Your friend Welles will either ruin you or make you famous Hargreaves, but I rather suspect it will be the latter. I don't know about you, but I would never have contemplated a woman as a detective in a crime story.' I said, 'Yes, but on reflection Agatha Christie has done well with Miss Marple, so it can be done.' As I fed a sheet of paper into my little typewriter he distracted me with, 'Friend Johnson is indeed very like the late lamented actor Hunter, is he not?' I agreed in an absent manner as I tapped out the first of my script changes. Holmes persisted with his interest, 'Do you, by chance, have any photographs of Hunter?' It so happened that I had a trade magazine that had run a tribute to Hunter with pictures. I found it and spread the appropriate pages upon the table for his perusal. He examined them as I resumed my typing, but I was to be interrupted again within a few minutes. Holmes called me over to the table and pointed a bony forefinger at one of the pictures. 'Hunter had a slight deformation to his left thumb.' I studied the picture and commented, 'Nothing of a kind that would be normally noticed very much. Why! Harold Lloyd had three fingers missing but few have ever commented on it. All the same, I'm a little surprised that it was not retouched in the picture.'

Interruptions seldom come singly, and sure enough within thirty minutes of recommencing my work, I was distracted again, though not by Holmes this time, but by a noise from Baker Street itself. The once sedate thoroughfare is even today of a quiet nature compared, for example, with the close by Edgware

Road, so I was a little surprised to see from the window a large and noisy group of people, mostly men, marching with banners. It was evidently some kind of anti-government unrest with trade union banners and the odd home-made 'hammer and sickle' flag. It was noisy and robust but seemingly fairly good-humoured. I prayed that it would remain so and not be of such a nature that could prompt a stable British administration to adopt McCarthy type panic measures. As the main banner-carrying group passed, other smaller knots of individuals followed, chanting and singing. One of these groups carried musical instrument cases but no banners. They were singing some kind of chant. Holmes looked at them with interest and said, 'Now that is interesting, Hargreaves. Do you not think, all things being equal, that the musical gentlemen should be playing their instruments in such a parade? Notice also how carelessly they handle their instrument cases. That's very significant, Hargreaves.' But I was tired of being distracted and thrust myself busily into my work, leaving

Holmes to continue to watch that passing parade of those who were far from enchanted with their government.

Several hours later, just when I thought that nothing else could occur to interrupt the emasculation of 'Walton', friend Hudson called for his rent. I had, on advice from Lyle Garrison, obtained a little volume known as a rent book. As he took the money and signed with a practised flourish, he glanced uneasily at Holmes. Then he asked, 'Everything 'tickety-boo', Mr. 'argreaves?' I assured him that everything was not only 'tickety-boo' but 'okay' as well. He returned the fountain pen to his breast pocket, nodded and departed.

After he had returned to his attic I turned to Holmes and said, 'You made no attempt to hide yourself, Holmes, and yet he made no allusion to your presence. Do you not find that surprising?' He chuckled, 'Not really my dear fellow, you see Hudson knows who and what I am, and has seen me many times, yet I get the impression that he is not entirely sure if others can see me. I believe he considers that he alone is haunted, and is not anxious to be thought of as insane until he can be quite sure of the validity in a wider sense of the 'Ghost of Baker Street'!' I reflected upon Hudson's past faint surprise when I had not complained to him concerning things that go bump in the night. My failure to complain about such things would doubtless have strengthened his suspicion that only he could see and hear the ghost of Sherlock Holmes.

My next visit to the studio was interesting, not just on account of the Orsonian revolution, but on account of a visit from Inspector Reynolds. He sidled up to me and involved me in a rather affable conversation, 'Well, Mr. Hargreaves, you will, I'm sure, be delighted to hear that I am not here to re-arrest Mr. Garrison, or indeed to arrest anyone, yourself included, but I put it to you that this is an unique setting in terms of the Craig murder.' Politely I asked why. He said, 'Oh! Of course there is no way that you could have known this, but all of those who were on Craig's list of so called subversives, have migrated to this studio and are present at this very moment! Garrison, yourself, Johnson, Miss Clovis and Orson Welles.' I was interested to note that he gave Orson alone his full name. Respect, irony or intimidation, I knew not which but noted one name was missing and said, 'How about Miss Shultz? She is also here.' He started, 'How could you know that, Mr. Hargreaves? Who has told you? Someone at the Yard?' I realised that I had made a serious blunder. 'Why no, but as the only other principal here I imagined your collection of names must have included hers.' He affected to take the point but I could see that he was suspicious. Orson saved the day for me. As director, whilst still in his laird's attire, he called a halt. 'Okay kids, take an hour and then we'll carry on from scene sixteen on the riverbank.' He gestured towards a collection of artificial reeds standing before a sky cloth, and lit an enormous corona. He used a Zippo just like mine, except that his managed to produce a blinding flash as his thumb spun the wheel. I figured it was some expensive gimmick that he had obtained from the Hollywood magic store — the one that Bert Wheeler had run for many years. I pretended to need to go into a huddle with Welles concerning the script, and that got me off the hook with Reynolds for a while so that I could have thoughts concerning my slip up. Reynolds went off to talk with Garrison and I told Orson all about it, but leaving out the part where I had got the information from Sherlock Holmes! Instead I said, 'A friend, a good friend, one that I cannot let down told me the names that were on the list of McCarthy suspects.' Orson considered, then said, 'Tell him that I told you the extra name.' I gasped, 'But Orson, that might make him suspect you. Why he might even arrest you!' Welles cocked an omnipotent eyebrow and boomed, 'He wouldn't dare!' Suspecting that Orson knew just what to say I took him at his word.

I caught Reynolds as he finished his conversation with Garrison. He said sternly, 'Our conversation was interrupted. Where does your friend Cyril

Raymond reside?' 'Reside, why I don't really know except that he spends most of his time in London. I believe he has another home on the Sussex coast somewhere.' He grunted, 'I see, and he is a close friend of yours?' I replied, 'Very close. He spends a lot of his time at my Baker Street rooms and stops overnight quite often.' He asked, 'How long have you actually known Mr. Raymond?' I faltered, 'About six weeks, but I have known of him for many years so our friendship developed more quickly than would be usual.' He was obviously intrigued, 'So you knew him by reputation. A reputation for being a bit of a character, I'll be bound?' I nodded, 'Well yes, his abilities and eccentricities have made him famous in certain circles.' All that I told him was, of course, perfectly true, for Cyril Raymond, under the name Sherlock Holmes had a world wide circle of admirers. Reynolds latched on to one of the words that I had used to describe my friend, 'Mr. Hargreaves, it is his seeming eccentricity which has prompted me to ask you these questions. I have absolutely no reason to suspect Mr. Raymond of any involvement in the case that I am investigating, none whatever, but I am human, even if I am a policeman, and so I cannot help but be intrigued by his persona. I can understand a man of eccentric nature lounging around indoors in an extremely elderly dressing gown, looking as if he was at death's door yet conversing in a manner sharp enough to contradict his appearance, but Mr. Hargreaves, I have caught sight of him in Regent's Park and other places, wearing that same faded red robe! Is this the normal behaviour of a man wealthy enough to have a home in Sussex as well as, we presume, some residence in London?' I could think of no reply but he saved me racking my brain further, 'No matter, his own affair, what! As a writer I have no doubt you cultivate eccentric characters in order to study them.' I was relieved when he let me off the hook so kindly and gracefully.

Then Lyle Garrison sidled up to me and said, 'Greg, Orson is not too keen on one of the six episodes. Do you think you could replace the one about the parson's dog with something stronger, within the next three or four days?' I am a writer, so I said, 'Yes, of course!' when I should have said, 'I'll try to'!

Holmes was amused at the account of my dialogue with Reynolds when I outlined it to him later. He chuckled as he said, 'Upon my word, Hargreaves, I really must keep my eyes open for the Inspector upon my future constitutionals, but just think what might have happened had his suspicions concerning me prompted him to attempt an arrest!'

At this point I was forced to try and cast the matter of Craig's murder and its attendant problems from my mind. I explained to Holmes that I had one last episode of 'Walton' to provide. I fed a sheet of paper into my trusty portable and began to work on the outline of a theme that had already suggested itself to my mind. I had decided that Miss Walton, and her friend the parson, would be fishing quietly from the weir at Sunbury when a police inspector would interrupt to seek her advice upon a local matter.

Lord Westcliffe would have disappeared from his study in his mansion under impossible circumstances. The study would, I decided, have a stone floor and seem to have no hiding places, being mainly just furnished with a collection of curios. I was not directly appealing to Holmes for help or advice, but I did cast the sheets of paper casually onto the table in a row rather than a pile, so that he could peruse them should the mood take him.

I had followed the rules of the game by first setting myself a problem, in the hope that I could solve it. Next I enlarged upon the theme, making the last person to see him alive being an elderly footman delivering to him a pot of tea and some scones, clearly still upon the table on a tray. Miss Walton would wish to interview the elderly footman but, of course, he would prove to be missing also, despite having been clearly seen emerging from the study having delivered the tray. At first as baffled as the viewer, Miss Walton would return to fishing in order to contemplate, and encounter one of those strokes of good fortune with which most detective fiction is peppered. She would hook not a tench or a rudd, but a wig of the type worn by footmen. A search of the surrounding countryside would yield livery and knee breeches and distinctive brown curly hairs within the wig would suggest that the noble Lord himself, rather than his elderly retainer had worn it. So in a flash of inspiration, suggested by her lucky find, Miss Walton would explain that Lord Westcliffe had emerged from his study wearing his footman's wig and livery, and no doubt using some of his acting ability. It would transpire that he wished to 'disappear' for reasons of debt, but what would he have done with the aged footman? Murdered him in order to purloin his livery? If so, what would he have done with the body?

Of course, before producing my 'big finish' I had to work out other matters to satisfy the sometimes critical television audience. For example, I asked myself, why did Lord Westcliffe not simply walk out of the big house and take himself off to the local railway station and from thence head for Victoria to embark upon a boat train? The answer could be that his creditors had mounted a watch with bailiffs and various process servers who would spot him decamping with the family jewel box! They would hardly pursue an elderly retainer evidently about some errand. It was beginning to fit together, but I had not yet answered the sixty-four thousand dollar question concerning what he had done with the body of the old footman that he had so cruelly slain to bring about this plan.

I glanced shyly in Holmes' direction. He was at last studying the row of neatly typed quarto sheets. He ran through a truly astonishing range of facial expressions — amusement, anger, cynicism and even pity.

So to my *grand finale*! I decided that the footman's body should be eventually discovered by the astute Miss Walton hidden in a suit of armour. Why had this not been suspected before? Well, the helmet had one of those visors which involves a built in grill, so flipping this had not revealed the footman's head on account of a piece of black material which had been placed over it. The several widths of metal would rise as one to a similar number of gaps, but the black material would just give the impression of a dark interior. Of course, Miss Walton's discoveries would allow the police to act more swiftly than might have been possible, thus enabling the apprehension of the wicked Lord Westcliffe!

'Well?' Holmes at first ignored my pathetic little voice of enquiry, but at length he took pity on me and said, 'I will not attempt to criticise the plot of the story for it is too ridiculous to merit serious discussion. The device where the body is revealed to be in the suit of armour may be possible but extremely unlikely . . . what if Lord Westcliffe was secretly addicted to alcohol and had a seven foot preserved grizzly bear standing upright and hollowed out completely so that it could be opened to reveal a man sized compartment intended to serve as his wine cellar?' I could see the wisdom in that and added, 'the sudden appearance in the study of a number of wine bottles on racks could add to the early mystery. Where had they suddenly appeared from and why?' He chuckled, 'It has more style than your suit of armour device, Hargreaves, but serves the purpose well. Otherwise I will not dwell upon the convenience of your lady angler hooking the wig, for stranger and even wilder pieces of good fortune have manifested themselves to me in the course of my career.'

Holmes continued, 'Just one genuine literary criticism then. Your story would seem more natural if Miss Walton poked her nose into police matters, much to their annoyance, rather than being asked to participate. This way, you can get a stronger finish when she discovers the body, bearing out a theory which others have scorned!' I could tell at once that Holmes' advice was sound and incorporated it into my final version of the script. Oh, that I could have typed the words 'By Greg Hargreaves and Sherlock Homes' on its title leaf! Alas, that would have been impractical for a variety of reasons and partially untrue, for Holmes had merely made suggestions. However, many a famous name has ended up on a title leaf as 'co-writer' on an even flimsier pretext. During the ensuing few days all of my energy was thrown into rewriting and perfecting the script, and in roughing out some ides for a possible second series, but as I worked the mystery of Craig and his murder kept creeping back into my mind and presenting me with a mystery more profound than any that Miss Walton might solve.

8

At some point during my entire absorption in 'Walton', Sherlock Holmes had evidently decided to take off and pursue his own interests. There were no good-byes, and I did not even notice that he had decamped so complete was my concentration with my work, but then, of course, the day came when I started to look around for Holmes and wonder just at what point he had departed.

It even occurred to me that he might have taken offence at my absorption even though none had been intended. Perhaps I would not see the 'Ghost of Baker Street' again, though I hoped with all my heart that I would. Meanwhile, however, I had to face the practicalities of what this would involve. It would mean that I would be deprived of the greatest detective ever, and the enormous value of his help in trying to clear up the question of who had murdered McCarthy's agent, which I needed to do for my own peace of mind. I had not been arrested, or even seriously suspected, it is true, but Garrison had, and he was not only someone that I liked and respected, but possibly the key to my establishment in Britain and the legality of my continued residence in that country. Therefore, Holmes or no Holmes, I determined to continue to investigate the crime.

It occurred to me that we might, both Holmes and I, have been concentrating our suspicions a little too single mindedly upon the names that we knew were on that infamous Craig list. With this thought, I decided to cast my net a little more widely. The names on the list, I figured, could be mere connections with whoever had committed the crime. Therapist Wardle fell into this category through his connection with Peppy Clovis, and although Holmes had consulted him briefly I thought I would try to dig deeper in that direction. It was easy enough to make an appointment with Wardle but far more difficult to know what tactics to adopt with him. I remember Holmes' mention of an enquiry concerning crocuses, which he thought might be an invitation to a coded reply. I mused upon this and eventually decided to grasp firmly at this straw.

When Professor John Wardle greeted me I said, 'Crocuses are out of season, are they not?' It was a shot in the dark but evidently I had made a hit! He gave me a keen look before guardedly saying, 'Bergen's partner must be disposed of.' I racked my brain. The only Bergen that came into my mind was an American ventriloquist who had made a big hit on radio and in the movies back in the thirties. I remembered that he had a dummy called Charlie McCarthy. Of course, he was referring to the Senator from Wisconsin! I decided to lead him on in the hope of hearing more. 'I'll clip him, I'll mow him down!' Fortunately Charlie's catch phrase had returned to my mind after so many years. That was evidently it. The correct response! I had been more than lucky and he relaxed. 'Do you have anything for me?' It was my turn to be guarded, 'Not really, except that whoever got Craig saved us a lot of trouble.' This was a shot to nothing. It could have blown everything for me, but it didn't and had been a chance worth taking for he said, 'That is right. It wasn't one of our people of course, but I weep no tears. We do not assassinate, as you know. Are you in touch with anyone over here yet?' I took the biggest chance of all and said, 'Peppy Clovis.' Rather more than ever to my surprise he did not react with anything but serenity saying, 'Yes, a grand girl, and she may yet effect the whole course of history of this country, but then, I do not need to tell you that.' I scarcely knew what to say and just waited for him to continue. 'The Government may fall very shortly, when it all comes out.'

I decided to change the direction of the conversation before I got into deeper water than my knowledge could support. When I tried to bring other names into the conversation I did not seem to strike any sort of responsive chord. I made my farewells to Wardle with the added assurance that I would be in touch with him again in the near future.

Back at Baker Street my mind reeled at the possible meaning of Wardle's words. He seemed to have made it clear that he was not really interested greatly in the Craig affair, and was probably quite without involvement in it. However, it was equally clear that he was involved with some sort of left wing conspiracy. What was it that he could be planning that would affect the well being of the British Government? I was, I realised, on thin ice here and would have to discuss the matter with the only person who might be able to tell me . . . Sherlock Holmes.

As it was Holmes continued to be conspicuous by his absence along with Hudson, who had not collected his rent for nearly two weeks. And so I continued to be alone with my dilemma. Daily I searched the newspapers for possible clues as to some problem concerning the Conservative Government of the day. There were stories and the usual reports of speeches by the Prime Minister, the Home Secretary and the guy in charge of the money. Nothing that I could read appeared to suggest any impending crisis or scandal. Some years later, long after the events of this story had ceased to occupy my mind, a scandal would erupt which would make my thoughts return to all those strange references to 'the crocuses'. A famous politician would be disgraced and the Government would fall, but more than a decade later than predicted.

Then, when I least expected it, a news story in *The Times* hit me right between the eyes. A headline, strong by that journal's standards, declared, 'WITCH HUNTER McCARTHY ESCAPES DEATH BY AN INCH'

The story which followed was less sensational but still couched in strong words.

From our New York reporter

Last night Joseph McCarthy, the Senator from Wisconsin, often referred to as 'the Witch Hunter', frequently derided in the world's press for his 'reds under the bed' image had an all but miraculous escape from an assassin's bullet. The Senator had settled into his lecture, 'The communist menace and the performing arts', when the silence that this had instilled, was shattered dramatically by the sharp report of an automatic weapon. McCarthy, though obviously shaken, moved to the right as if from instinct. (I am tempted to remind readers that he has been moving in that direction for years). The bullet expelled from the weapon was soon afterwards discovered embedded in the lectern behind which he had been standing.

A scuffle in the auditorium ensued and I saw a rather bizarre figure in what appeared to be a faded red dressing gown frantically drawing attention to another man who was still brandishing the pistol. This evident assassin, his coat collar upturned and hat pulled well down, then fired the revolver at point blank range at the man in the dressing gown. What happened next was hard to believe and the reader may be forgiven for doubting the veracity of my words, but from where I stood it appeared to me that the bullets (there were two reports) could not possibly have missed their mark, and yet appeared to have no effect whatsoever upon their target.

The assassin escaped into the crowd as the police made their way towards the spot where he had stood. Others turned towards the man in the crimson robe. My job is to report the events exactly as I see them. With this in mind I promise the reader that the man in the dressing gown vanished as I watched him unblinkingly.

Please do not misunderstand my words, for I do not insult your intellect by suggesting that he faded-from view or disappeared in a flash like something at Maskelyne's mysteries . . . no, but at one second he was there and the next he was gone. Later I questioned a number of people who had actually stood next to or around his person. They were all of one voice that one moment he of the crimson robe was there, and the next he was not. All were sure that he had been shot twice at waist level without effect, other than to cause him to vanish seemingly into thin air.

However, this comment upon the more sensational aspect of the event should not deter me from continuing my report upon this attempted assassination of one of America's most colourful and controversial figures. No arrests were made despite a frantic search of the auditorium and its surrounds. Naturally the police are still investigating the incident. It is doubtless without point for them to search for a small man with his hat pulled down and a probably stuck-on ginger moustache. Likewise they are not seeking the man in the dressing gown, save to congratulate him, for according to onlookers, his swift action saved McCarthy's life. Not everyone, of course, would wish to congratulate him! As for Senator McCarthy himself, afterwards he commented, 'The fanatic's attempt upon my life only illustrates for all to see the lengths to which these people will go in order that free speech should not be heard. Who do I think he was? Why he may have been a hired assassin in the pay of the Soviets, but I think it more likely that we are dealing here with an American citizen, a communist or fellow traveller, whose action has made my point for me more strongly than I could have myself had I been able to finish my oration. The reds have failed to silence Joe McCarthy and unwittingly done him a great big favour!'

The Senator seemed somewhat disinterested when questioned concerning the man who had saved his life.

He said, 'Maybe he was wearing a bullet proof vest, but if so, why? Anyway I don't much admire the choice he made concerning the colour of his robe. Pink it was, you say? Well I guess many a pinko might think that the reds were going too far!' When told that the man appeared to be somewhat emaciated, he commented, 'Sure he did . . . all pinkos are sick!'

Rest assured that I will continue to report upon any fresh aspect of this very strange occurrence.

I laid down the paper as if in a daze. Clearly Sherlock Holmes had taken himself off to New York, which whilst it explained his absence, scarcely made clear how he had known about the proposed assassination, or why he had decided to save the far from sympathetic character who had been the target.

I muttered (audibly, evidently) 'Why should Holmes want to save McCarthy?'

I was unnerved when the familiar incisive voice replied, 'Elementary, my dear Hargreaves, for in tracking down the killer of Craig, I had no wish to stand by and watch a fellow human slain. I have no particular feelings concerning the theories of Marx or Lenin, considering them to be just that, merely theories, and neither do I applaud the words and actions of Joseph McCarthy whom I consider to be an extremely dangerous man. However, I cannot stand by and do nothing in the full knowledge that murder is about to be committed. The would-be assassin evaded capture but then this was my intention, and unimportant anyway because, now that I know their identity, their eventual capture is assured. We are nearing the point where we can prove the innocence, or otherwise, of your friend, Garrison.'

I started at his words and his eyes twinkled as he continued, 'Oh! Come, Hargreaves, you must return to an impartial view at this point in time. By the by, how did you get on with our other friend, Wardle?'

I started again, 'How did you know that I had been to see him taking into account your own involvement of the past week?'

He smiled and replied, 'I at once noticed the small tear at the bottom of your left trouser leg. It's consistent with the nail which protrudes at the base of the clients' side of Wardle's desk. You will note that I have an almost identical imperfection.'

He made an indicating gesture with a bony forefinger, while I tried to recognise the tear among so many imperfections. I meant to ask him what would happen when his existing clothes were completely ruined, but never seemed to get the chance. I wondered though if he had not already decided that I had visited Wardle before making this deduction, but I suppose a great detective is entitled to cheat now and then, even when he is a mere apparition!

To my surprise Holmes listened to the account of my visit to the therapist with a minimum of interest. In fact, eventually he held up an admonishing hand saying, 'You have discovered nothing new, Hargreaves, but you have merely confirmed certain suspicions of my own about Wardle. Your lady friend, Peppy

Clovis, appeared to be an extremely well adjusted young woman and not at all a candidate, past or present, for Wardle's treatment. The two of them are connected. She is his agent, seeking suitably eccentric or unhappy people of means to become involved with him. She reminded me of an adventuress connected with a case of mine many years ago. She was engaged in luring wealthy men to become involved in card games in which her male accomplice fleeced them of large sums of money. She has that way with her. She looked at my tattered robe and strange appearance, and assumed that I must be a very wealthy eccentric to get away with such bizarre behaviour (you are, after all, a man with connections like Lyle Garrison and Orson Welles!). Armies have been defeated and governments have fallen though involvement with such people.'

Holmes seemed suddenly to be in an expansive mood and switched the conversation to a member of the Walton cast, Wayne Johnson. He said, 'Ever since you showed me the photographs of James

Hunter, I have been intrigued with the coincidence of events which have allowed Johnson to practically step into Hunter's shoes. Examine all the facts that surround this situation. Hunter was in trouble with McCarthy and evidently took his own life. The actor Wayne Johnson known to be near enough in appearance to he hired to finish Hunter's last film progressed as far as to eventually get the roles that Hunter would have played. Not only were they alike, but also Johnson proved to be an equally fine actor, yet without any past record of brilliance. He has the added advantage of having no problem with McCarthy. I have noticed that both actors shared an unusual characteristic, a malformation of the left thumb. This takes the situation away from being one of fate and coincidence. The man who passes as Wayne Johnson is, in fact, James Hunter. It was Johnson who did the vanishing act, with Hunter taking on his persona and therefore being quickly able to rebuild his career under a fresh name. He is careful to play parts which require him to wear wigs, which alter his appearance. His baldness is caused by the diligent use of a razor rather than being natural.'

I was to learn no more concerning his examination of the photograph. Instead I was to be subjected to a barrage of questions concerning Lyle Garrison, Winni Shultz and inevitably Peppy Clovis. 'Aside from the fact that she is attractive and has good teeth, what do we know of her?' I told him what I could. 'Like most starlets she came on the scene with a protector, rather like Marion and Hearst, or Jane and Hughes. The guy who promoted her was a sort of minor gangster really, a chum of George Raft's, but she dropped him, even before he ended up in Sing Sing.'

Of course, I realised that he was lining up a row of suspects rather more in the tradition of Hercules Poirot than that of Sherlock Holmes. He even asked questions about Orson, or rather he asked me to give him some general idea of his background, hoping perhaps to hear something that might not have been public knowledge. I began, 'Wealthy parents, privately educated and originally destined to be a painter. He was on a sketching tour of southern Ireland when, travelling with a donkey cart, he arrived in Dublin where he ran out of money. Michael McClairmore took a fancy to him and gave him a part in a play. This turned him into an actor and he quickly gained fame on stage and more importantly on radio in the States. He produced and narrated a radio version of H.G. Wells' *War of the Worlds* and scared the pants off the whole nation. Listeners took the fake reports seriously. He went to Hollywood and made friends and enemies in equal numbers with his film *Citizen Kane*. Three wives, all beautiful women, and dozens of lady friends. Oh, yes, and he once had his own magical circus in which he performed illusions nightly. At the moment he is considered difficult to handle by producers and so he roams the world appearing on the stage and playing guest roles in other people's movies. He has a room full of scripts and projects that he wants to direct and he is trying to raise the dollars to make a start on these. To him Joe McCarthy is just a minor irritant as you have possibly guessed.'

At this point a diversion occurred when I switched on the television set to get the news transmission. As I had hoped there was an item about the attempted McCarthy assassination. There it was much as described by *The Times* correspondent, with the Senator having his angry oration interrupted by a sharp report and his sudden lurch to his right. There was then some rather shaky camera work as the small figure in the pulled down hat and sporting a walrus moustache appeared to be firing his revolver at an empty space! At first I thought that Holmes' non-appearance was the result of some kind of brilliant censorship, the technicalities of which even I, as a movie man, did not understand. But the BBC reporter explained that, 'Witnesses spoke afterwards of a strange figure in a red dressing gown which ruined the would-be assassin's aim and evoked his rage to the extent that two more shots were fired, point blank, at the man in question. As you will see, however, from this slow motion replay, no figure in a dressing gown is to be seen, just a lurch to the left from the gunman and then the seeming expulsion of two more shots which evidently did not find their mark'. The announcer then went on to talk about the extreme weather conditions in the West Country, and, at that point, I switched off. Holmes' face was about as animated as a ghost gets. He said, 'We have made an interesting discovery, Hargreaves, concerning a new talent of mine, if it can be called such, the fact that my image cannot be captured by a camera unless, of course, this was some kind of a freak occurrence. I suppose I will need to go to a photographic studio to assure myself of the answer.' I had the solution, and that solution lay somewhere in the depths of my overnight bag. It had been purchased as the answer to all my dreams, and as yet had never been used. It was a 'Land Camera', the very latest photographic marvel, and the eighth wonder of the world. With this brilliant invention, one could take a picture, press a button and the finished print would emerge from the camera like magic. At least it was almost as good as that. In fact a black image emerged from the camera, which given two or three minutes would develop into a picture which one would then 'fix' with a sponge stick charged with hypo. Today instant picture cameras are smaller, less complicated, quicker and more of a marvel. But back in the fifties that 'Land Camera' was a bit of a miracle. It took me a while to get used to handling the camera and at last I could produce an excellent picture of the sideboard. Knowing that I could do this, I stood Holmes in front of it and placed a potted plant behind him. In theory, the picture that emerged would show Holmes and parts of the sideboard with the plant being completely obscured. In fact, the picture showed only the sideboard and the plant! Holmes was intrigued, and I was amazed that he had not until now experienced the fact that he could not be captured by a camera lens. It was evidently one of the characteristics of being a ghost!

Holmes, after having insisted on my

production of a vast amount of tobacco smoke, made an interesting suggestion. He led gently into this with an enquiry, 'When, Hargreaves, do you imagine the first of your screenplays will be broadcast if that is the correct expression?' I told him, 'June the fourth, at seven thirty in the evening.' He was thoughtful for a while eventually saying, 'How would it be if you were to invite a number of the principals involved with you in the production to a small function here at Hudson House? Keep the number you invite within very compact bounds . . . scarcely more than those who are upon our list of suspects. You can avoid any complaint by Hudson by bribing him with an invitation!' I said that I thought that I could arrange such a modest function, but added, 'It had better be held rather late in the evening, perhaps at around ten clock.' Holmes nodded and said, 'Good, and I suggest that you might want to also invite Inspector Reynolds.' I was a little surprised at this suggestion, 'Why the Inspector, Holmes?' He chuckled and said, 'In the event that I have by then solved the mystery, he could be very useful for the apprehension of the murderer. Come, my dear Hargreaves, you of all people should know that it is done that way in all the best murder mystery stories.' I said, 'But Holmes, this is not a story that we are involved in, and I cannot recall your 'Boswell', Doctor Watson, penning any such device for the conclusion of any of your famous cases.' He said, 'All this is so, but then it is my first really important assignment since I ceased a more active existence, and the theatrical aura of the device suits my present day mood! Come, Watson, I mean Hargreaves, let us have a little fun for once. I was always far too serious in life!'

It was now obvious to me that Holmes really did believe that he would have solved the mystery of the identity of Craig's killer by June the fourth. He had not really made clear if he considered that the Craig murderer and the would-be assassin of Joseph McCarthy were one and the same. If they were this would, of course, eliminate the female persons on our present list, unless . . . The sudden bizarre thought occurred to me that the attempt upon the Senator could have been made by a woman disguised as a man! The reports had, after all, suggested a 'small person' which would certainly eliminate Orson, but then I could not believe that he was capable of killing Craig, or anyone else for that matter. However, Holmes had most particularly suggested his invitation to what I was fast beginning to think of as 'the great murder mystery climax'. For that particular evening I said no more to Holmes upon the subject.

On the following morning I typed five or six invitations to my little shindig and posted them in the bright red cylinder at the top of Baker Street. I was fast becoming used to the strange British ways and highly original names and references.

I posted all the invitations, except those for Inspector Reynolds and Hudson, the former of whom I preferred to telephone. He was surprised, of course, but rather liked the idea of being invited. I played down any suggestion that I wanted him to mix business with pleasure, making the invitation a purely social one. He accepted unreservedly except to suggest that I might forgive him if he did not appear exactly at the stroke of ten. 'Business could intervene, Mr. Hargreaves, but rest assured that I will be with you as soon after that time as I can make it.'

I got written answers from Winni, Peppy, Orson (on Claridges note paper), Wayne and Lyle Garrison. There were fortunately a few days to go before June the fourth during which time I could prepare for the 'Walton' celebration. I laid in a few bottles of the least expensive champagne that I could locate and a whole lot of the nearest thing to pretzels that were available, various crisps and some peanuts. Something a little more solid would be required for them to eat, so I bought some canned sausages in brine to combat my icebox problem. I needed some rolls in which to serve them, but I decided to leave their purchase until the day of the function so that they would be fresh and not too hard. I got in a couple of bottles of gin and some

Vermouth to make Martinis, and prayed that I would be able to keep them all fed and watered for two or three hours. I had decided to cast Holmes' reason for suggesting the function right out of my mind lest I betray some ulterior motive by word or deed. After all, even if the 'Ghost of Baker Street' did not fulfil his intention, the evening could well be entertaining.

During the days that followed, right up to the day of the party, I saw very little of Sherlock Holmes, who was evidently following activities of his own. I knew that he was hard at work on the case, if such it could be called. I remembered the feeling of resentment that I had harboured during that time when he was in New York, little dreaming the important nature of his activities and assuming him to be hanging around Simpsons, or walking in the park. I would not, of course, misjudge him further, or make the same mistake again. I decided that my shindig to celebrate the first showing of 'Walton' should have some kind of theme. What better than one of angling? I bought a few cheap fishing poles and started to decorate the living room at Hudson House. I bought some floats made out of porcupine quills to replace swizzle sticks for the drinks, but I wanted something a little more impressive to form some kind of background to it all.

With this in mind I remembered passing a novelty store that I had seen on New Oxford Street during one of my strolls around London. It was what, back home, would have been called a magic store, a family business with 'L. Basingstoke and Co. Established 1893' above the door. The window was crammed with a vast number of tricks and novelties, from a gadget for beheading people without having to go to jail, through vanishing dice and the like, right down to packets of trick soot and imitation dog poo. I could not see into the shop because the glass door was obscured with magic booklets secured by bulldog clips and suspended from threads. They had exciting looking covers illustrated with rabbits leaping from stovepipe hats, and playing cards cascading from the left

hand of a demonic figure into his right.
These pamphlets had arresting titles, such
as, *Show Me Another* and *That's a good
one!* As I opened the door to enter there
was a tinkle made by one of those bell
gadgets that candy stores used to have
way back when, and inside there was a
vista of the kind that I had not seen since
childhood when a magical uncle took me
to Martinks in New York.

I surveyed with wonderment the rows
of implements for 'presto chango' that
filled the showcases from floor to ceiling.
There were strange looking glass boxes,
tripods with antique ball and claw feet, a
metal star with a playing card at its every
point, cones, caddies and mystic cloths
and a pack of cards that were so big that
the largest hand could not have con-
cealed one of them. Aside from Martinks
this was the first magic shop that I had
been in aside from a slick businesslike
affair in Hollywood, which had preserved
no atmosphere and so did not really
count.

Behind the counter stood a bespec-
tacled little guy with dark hair brushed

flat back. He was middle aged and had a rather brusque 'whadda ya want?' kind of manner (that was, I would later find, all you got until you knew him better). A cork tipped cigarette hung from his lips, occasionally depositing ash upon the waistcoat of his otherwise neat blue serge three-piece suit. I politely enquired, 'Do you have anything to do with fish?' Almost without hesitation, he produced a paper scoop of imitation French fries from beneath the counter asking, 'How about a few chips?' I laughed. He didn't. It was his business and no longer amused him. I said, 'Great gag, but what I want are a few novelty items to enliven a fishing party.' He took a fresh cigarette from a packet labelled 'Black Cat' and lit it from the dying embers of the one he took from his mouth. He took a neat white handkerchief from his display pocket and poked a depression into it with his thumb, into this he pushed the still glowing butt, then he shook out the handkerchief showing it to be unharmed, and returned it to his display pocket. He did this as an aside, prior to bringing forth a yard square of silk, beautifully printed with a huge depiction of a tropical fish. He folded it down small and told me that it was 'ideal for loading'. I didn't know what he meant, but despite it being rather expensive for something that I would use only once I bought it. I asked him why it cost so much and he replied, 'It's on account of rent, rates, light, heat, income tax, purchase tax, surtax, super tax and excess profit charges!'

The shopkeeper also sold me a rubber fish, and four glass bowls. These could be instantly populated by live fish when filled with water. When I dared to ask how this was possible he said, 'Read the instructions!' I started to stagger towards the door with my purchases balanced like a juggling feat. Extending a mitten clad hand for me to shake, he ruined it all, for I had to put down the tower of boxed fishbowls in order to comply. He said, 'My name is George Basingstoke, even though I'm a Londoner!' I didn't get the joke for days.

I took a cab back to Baker Street where

I played with my purchase, filling the bowls with water and reading the instructions. The bowls had thick plated metal rims around their neck apertures and there were secret compartments in these which hid live goldfish until the tug upon a thread released them into the water. The fish were kept alive by being hidden in contact with pieces of damp sponge. It was complicated and difficult to use, especially when, like me, you didn't have any goldfish!

My next job was to seek out a pet store where I might be able to purchase some goldfish. I found one in George Street, another Aladdin's cave of a shop where an elderly man in a dust coat sold me a dozen tiny gold and silver fish for 'a tanner each'. It was when I realised that a 'tanner' was only about a dime that I decided to get that many. The old guy threw in a tin can for me to transport them in, and for an extra 'bob' I got a tube of fish food. Alas, most of the fish did not live to see their first meal and my experiments with my magic fish bowls caused me to stroll to and from the pet store several times. However, the silken banner with the fishy decal looked good when I pinned it to the wall between the Turkish slipper and the portrait of 'the woman'.

9

The day of June the fourth finally dawned. Even if I was not actually awakened at the moment of dawn breaking, by my own standards I was early to the breakfast table, and therefore somewhat amazed to find Sherlock Holmes already sitting there, I was about to say 'looking like death warmed up' but the phrase when applied to him has a certain redundancy. He greeted me, 'Hargreaves, forget about that dreary bowl of 'Force' (he had caught up with the breakfast cereals of the twenties but not yet those of the fifties!) and light up a Chesterfield, or Lucky Strike, if you cannot face a pipe at this hour.' I thanked him for sparing me a lung full of 'Scottish Mixture' at seven in the morning and obligingly blew the cigarette smoke in his direction. I had not seen my ghostly colleague for several days and was naturally anxious to hear of anything that he might have discovered which could prove positively the identity of Craig's killer and McCarthy's would-be slayer, and perhaps clarify if they were one and the same.

In his own time, prompted by my enquiries, Holmes said, 'My dear fellow, everything in its turn. You have made all the arrangements that we have already discussed, and I can see from the *décor* that you have acted upon your own initiative as well. Obviously you have visited the premises of Mr. Basingstoke. The several dead goldfish in your dustbin area should have alerted me to that, for I was a regular patron of the late Lewis Basingstoke who had premises in the East End in my day.' I said, 'I did not know that you had an interest in conjuring.' He replied, 'Nor had I, or have to this day, but Basingstoke used to sell me a great many useful requisites for purposes of disguise. False noses, darkening cosmetics and things of that kind. Oh, and false whiskers of which he had the finest selection in London. Aside from all this I noticed the goblin trademark which is engraved upon the rim of the metal collar of one of your fish bowls.'

Holmes then told me that he had not been idle since our last meeting and had been 'making enquiries in my own strange way'. 'The speed of air travel made it possible for me to eliminate most of the coincidence that both Johnson and Hunter should have the same malformation of the left thumb. Such a great likeness of appearance intrigued my curiosity. Add to this the convenient disappearance of Hunter and the advancement of Johnson's career as a consequence, and you have a strange story indeed.'

I started, 'You do not suggest that Wayne murdered Hunter surely?' He replied, 'Not at all, this would have been impossible because the man who passes so easily as Wayne Johnson is, in fact, James Hunter as I suspected. You see it was Johnson 'the small part actor and double' who died in that car crash which occurred so close to Hunter's home. Hunter was the first on the scene and the opportunity to disappear and start afresh with a new persona occurred to him. After all, he had been ruined by McCarthy's attentions and had nothing to lose. I deduced that he placed Johnson's body in his own car and pushed it over the cliff. The car exploded and burned when it reached the ground, with the body being charred beyond recognition. But enough artefacts would have survived to connect the body with Hunter. He then had only to sit beside the battered car that had hit a tree. An inquest would not have found the circumstances suspicious, with Johnson having nothing to gain, they would think, from Hunter's death.'

Foolishly I said, 'But surely Holmes, this is all theoretical is it not?' Holmes turned his gimlet eyes onto me, 'I have, of course, been to the scene of the tragedy and investigated. (It is not difficult for me to make such excursions you know). The police had been disinterested in any examinations of the surrounding road surface. After all, they had found a dazed Johnson (as they believed him to be) beside a damaged car registered in his name, and another car evidently containing Hunter's body. Hunter had Johnson's wallet with his identification papers, but had they examined that little used road surface they would have found, as I did, the unmistakable signs of a car having been pushed over the cliff . . . footprints between the tyre tracks, deeply sunk to indicate the difficulty of this task. I doubt if many cars had been there since the day of the tragedy. Even after so long I had been able to read these signs, and I'll wager they will be there until an unusually wet season alters their contours. Sometimes, Hargreaves, a man is presented with a situation with great advantage to him, yet where time is the essence. Changing identification papers and pushing the car over the cliff may have been performed almost instinctively, but it would have been too late to regret these rash acts by the time the authorities arrived, which would have been a matter of just a few minutes. The burning vehicle would have alerted the police.'

It was some minutes before I spoke again, my mind trying to adjust to what I had just been informed. Eventually I enquired, 'Do you intend to go public on this or will you sit on it?' Holmes was irritated by my words, 'Really, Hargreaves, I do wish you would learn to speak English. I imagine your unfamiliar phrase is intended to enquire if I mean to remain silent concerning the affair of Hunter and Johnson? The answer is that I do. I see no harm in remaining silent on the subject, and equally I cannot visualise the practicability of my giving evidence in a court of law, even in your country. Name: Sherlock Holmes. Residence: late of 221B Baker Street, London. Occupation: retired detective. Present status: Ghost! No, my dear fellow, there is an adage concerning the advisability of allowing a slumbering canine to continue to snore, and I suggest that you keep your own counsel on the matter as well.'

I said, 'I am going to continue to refer to Hunter as Johnson, even if I now know that the reverse is true, just to avoid confusion. O.K. Holmes? So we can cross Johnson off our list of suspects can we not?' Holmes shook his head, 'Come,

Hargreaves, you are confusing two issues. I have said that I do not think that the real Wayne Johnson was murdered, but this does not mean that Hunter, very well, Wayne Johnson as we now know him, is innocent of the crime of unlawfully killing Lionel Craig. However, let us leave the confusing actor out of the equations for the moment and consider our other listed suspects. We next come to the question of Mr. Lyle Garrison.' I said, 'I was hoping that he would be the very first to be cleared of all suspicion.' He said, 'Unfortunately, as the number one suspect he might be the most difficult to prove innocent. He had motive and, as far as we can tell, the opportunity to commit the crime. As you colonials would say, he has no convincing alibi. We have also to consider the threatening letter which he evidently sent to Craig. (He caught the flash of my eye.) Hold your horses, Hargreaves, for was it not I myself who suggested that he may well be telling the truth when he denied sending, let alone writing it. I suspect that the new photographic copying process produced the letterhead upon which it was written as I told you earlier, and his signature could well have been forged, but these are possibilities, nay probabilities, yet even so they by no means prove his innocence.' I was concerned for my livelihood quite aside from my concern for Garrison as a likeable colleague. I asked, 'Then how must we go about finding fresh proofs of his innocence?' Holmes said, 'We must take another route towards preventing his re-arrest.' He sat back in his chair and placed the tips of his all but translucent fingers together in what I had learned to accept as a characteristic pose. He continued, 'If we cannot prove him innocent then what we must do is more than obvious. We have only to find the real criminal and prove his guilt beyond question, so with this in mind let us continue to run a finger down our list. Please do not fidget, Hargreaves, but do make yourself some coffee, if you wish to, before we continue.'

I did as he bade, gratefully, and having made it, I poured the heaven sent black steaming liquid first into a pot, then into a cup and finally, eagerly, into my mouth. Coffee, hot, black and strong is to me what milky weak tea is to the British. I returned my large thick china cup to its saucer and leant forward to catch his every word. He said, 'The actress, Miss Winni Shultz, would at first thought be automatically eliminated through her petite build. She does not have the muscular ability to have killed Craig, especially in the manner in which it was done. However, she might have muscular allies and was certainly on Craig's list, as was Miss Clovis. Ah! Now here we have a rather more robust candidate with enough strength to have herself carried out the deed, especially if the victim were to be taken by surprise. He was not robust and Miss Clovis has this rather suspicious association with the psychiatric charlatan, John Wardle. Certainly I suspect them of collusion in activities subversive and she may be the only name which deserves to be on that infamous list of Craig's. As for your friend Orson Welles, I continue to view him as a suspect because nothing is impossible at this stage, and moreover, he would be furious if I did not consider him! Remember he told us that he was annoyed that he was not called before McCarthy's hearings despite doing everything but wave a red flag under the Senator's nose?' I agreed, 'Orson as an actor only plays forceful roles on stage, screen or in life; he would always go for the main event. If he were going to murder anyone it would have been McCarthy himself rather than his hired creep!' I suppose it was the writer in me that suddenly put a brilliant idea into my mind. A film about the rise and fall of McCarthy with Orson playing the Senator from Wisconsin! McCarthy was, at that moment in time, still rising, but I knew that he would fall, as he of course, eventually did. Orson never did play that part, though years later he would play a crooked police chief with McCarthy type undertones.

The writer in me makes me want to say 'the witching hour arrived', but of course that hour was more than a hundred and twenty minutes away when I started to look for my first guests to arrive. Winni Shultz arrived first and I seated her a fair distance from where Holmes was lounging. I plied her with cocktails and, of course, she noticed that Holmes was not drinking, but we passed it off as part of his health regime, which she knew about anyway. I asked her if she had seen the first 'Walton' episode, which Holmes and I had watched ealier that evening, the former with a rather detached air. She said, 'Yes, Greg, but I confess to having had a teensy weenie little preview. What did you think of it, Greg?' I nodded, and Holmes did the same when she looked directly at him. I felt a bit miffed that she had been treated to a preview, which I, as the scriptwriter had been denied! I said, 'I thought it was a good enough first episode to hook a few viewers for the series.' Holmes became aware that a short silence meant that he was expected to put in his ten cents worth. He said, 'I thought it compared quite favourably with that which I have seen before upon the television.' Knowing how little he had watched television, and his strange tastes when he did, made me consider this compliment as a back handed one.

Next to arrive was Lyle Garrison who was his usual kindly and genial self, despite the cloud which hung over him. He noticed the overpriced silken portrait of a fish at once and complimented me on my topicality of *décor*. He kissed Winni on the cheek and waved a hand in greeting to Holmes, saying, 'Now had your friend been here on that occasion which we will not discuss, things might have been different!' But I knew he was kidding, and also that he was not going to hold my minor nervous breakdown, as he saw it, against me. A considerable interval elapsed before the arrival of the next guest which Winni filled with a very amusing anecdote saying, 'Wow, when you hold a party you really to go town, Greg! It reminds me of a time in Hollywood when a famous director invited me to a party at his beautiful home in Beverly Hills.'

By eleven the others had all arrived, including Inspector Reynolds and Hudson, who true to form, brandished my rent book and would not be seated until I had handed him his money. He signed for it with his fountain pen which had a transparent section of the kind which allowed one to see just how much ink remained in the reservoir. I felt sorry for the poor little guy, anxious to impress with a gadget which was a novelty at the time of its purchase, which must have been twenty years before. Orson, of course, made an entrance, so theatrical that it drew a round of applause!

We sat around, sipping the drinks that I kept in circulation and, as so often happens on such an occasion, an impromptu show materialised. Wayne (as I had to remember to call him) gave some brilliant impersonations, including John Wayne, James Stewart and Clark Gable. In his introductions he mentioned that he had been given an unfair opportunity to study each of them when acting as their doubles. Holmes nodded his approval, catching my eye. (We both realised that this was untrue but admired his artful enterprise). He finished his turn with a wicked satire of Orson, stuffing a pillow under the casual jacket that he was wearing. No one laughed more than Welles himself. When it was Orson's turn to entertain us, he treated us to a series of card tricks that, although of a fairly simple nature, were presented with all that personal magnetism for which he was famed. Then suddenly he looked uncomfortable and a huge damp area started to develop on one side of his body. He said, 'Darn it, that wretched creature has peed in my pocket!' He fished the tiny rabbit from the huge side pocket of his jacket and dropped it gently enough on to my best mat, where the startled little creature blinked and finished performing his call of nature. Orson laughed hugely saying, 'I was going to pull it out of someone's hat as my *pièce de résistance*!'

Peppy Clovis, though, was the hit of the evening. She disappeared from the room for a moment or two and reappeared wearing a bowler hat, an overcoat and a ginger moustache. She gave us several verses of the Victorian music hall song, *Burlington Bertie*. She added several risqué verses of her own to the original as she marched up and down in the male top gear and false moustache. Her figure struck some sort of chord in my memory. Holmes caught my eye and I contrived to pass near to him. As I did so he whispered, 'Remember the gunman in the newsreel?' He was right of course. The height and stance were correct, as was the ginger moustache.

Assuming that Holmes would have spoken his accusations aloud if he wanted them made known, I tried to carry on as if I had not learned anything for the moment, even enticing Inspector Reynolds to take the floor. He obliged with a far from poor recitation of Edgar Allen Poe's *The Raven*. I produced my goldfish to very little effect and Hudson sang *The Man who Broke the Bank at Monte Carlo* in an excruciating tenor. It was left to Holmes to save the evening. I only sprang it on my ghostly friend because I could tell from his manner that he wished to be called upon. (Telepathy if you like, but I am sure that he and Watson had an even sharper rapport). I introduced, 'Our final turn . . . Mr. Cyril Raymond!'

Curiously enough there was a fair measure of applause. Holmes had made himself popular with my other guests as much through his obvious eccentricity as anything else. (Who but Cyril Raymond would turn up at a party in his every day, faded and torn, red dressing gown. Indeed, who but he would wear it at any time come to that?) He cleared his throat and began, 'Ladies and Gentlemen, I would like to give you a few demonstrations of a clairvoyant nature . . . ' For the next ten minutes he astounded his audience by telling each of them facts about themselves that he could not seemingly have possibly known. I soon realised that telepathy or clairvoyance had absolutely nothing to do with it and he was simply applying his famous 'methods.' He knew what mode of transport each had used, told Peppy that she had changed her mind twice concerning her choice of dress, and Lyle Garrison that he thought about calling in his apologies but had decided to come after all at the last minute. Visits to dentists, shopping expeditions and family gatherings were all commented upon to great effect. I realised that it was all elementary to Cyril Raymond. His spellbound audience started to shoot questions at him; 'Where was I last Friday night?', 'Name the winner of the big race next Saturday' and so on. Some questions he was able to answer with surprising alacrity, while others he dealt with in the spirit with which they had been intended. Then it happened, and it was Inspector Reynolds who dropped the bombshell.

'Who killed Lionel Craig?' He delivered his question with the mocking air of one who believed himself to be a master of satire, but the mockery left his expression when Holmes said, 'I will answer you by allowing my friend, Greg Hargreaves, to write it upon a scrap of paper which will be folded. You may read it when I give you the word to do so. Be so good, Hargreaves, as to take up the pad and pencil from the coffee table, and write upon it that which I tell you.' I did as he commanded and he whispered a name in my ear. I started at its utterance but decided to go along with his little joke. I wrote quickly then folded the paper and handed it to the Inspector who grunted and held the scrap betwixt finger and thumb aloft as if wishing its isolation. The Inspector smiled and said to Holmes, 'Come, Mr. Raymond, you have committed yourself, for whilst you may delay my reading of that which you have written, read it I eventually will! At least give us some sort of a clue, a *résumé* of possibilities. After all, everyone whose name appears upon Craig's list is with us right now.'

Holmes' eyes sparkled with a 'the game's afoot' type of glint, all but animating his gaunt features. He said, 'I will begin with Mr. Lyle Garrison. Whilst convinced of his innocence I could not prove it, so I had to prove the guilt of another suspect in order to clear his name.' Reynolds almost snapped, 'So the name on this paper is not Mr. Garrison's?' Holmes shook his head and continued, 'Neither is it that of Mr. Wayne Johnson. I'm not sure how his name got onto Craig's list but it certainly should not have been there. Anything that

I can detect concerning Mr. Johnson is of no interest to a Scotland Yard inspector, I assure you.' I was relieved at this statement by Holmes for I considered it unlikely that Reynolds would pursue him on any matter unconnected with the death of Craig. Johnson's face showed his gratitude and that he realised that Holmes knew his secret.

Holmes, in his continuing role of mind reader and detective said, 'A far from likely candidate is Miss Shultz, while our host, Mr. Greg Hargreaves, has an airtight proof of being far from the crime scene at the time in question.' Reynolds snapped, 'That is not quite as I see it, but do continue, Mr. Raymond.' Holmes said, 'Mr. Orson Welles has the physical strength and protean abilities to have been seriously considered. Whatever alibi he might establish would scarcely hold water as he has more than once used the device of allowing a friend of similar build to lead pursuers away from his scene of activity . . . '

I started at this and could not prevent myself from flying to Orson's defence.

'Holmes! Raymond! That is unworthy of you, for was it not you who suggested this mode of operation so that Orson might elude the bailiff, and thus be able to keep an important engagement?' Holmes looked mockingly at me and replied, 'There is no proof that Mr. Welles had not previously employed the device and felt my suggestion of it to be a gift from the Gods. After all, he would expect a reaction to his antics to be exactly as yours have been. No pray, do not look at the paper yet!' The Inspector hesitated before deciding not to follow his urge to examine Holmes' prediction. Orson was patently amused by the situation that placed him at its centre. He said, tongue in cheek, 'I suppose I was also the five-foot guy with the ginger moustache who tried to shoot 'reds under the bed', Joe?' Reynolds rounded smartly on him, 'The two assassins were not necessarily one and the same.'

'Let us now consider the possibilities of Miss Clovis.' Now that the shadow of guilt had been removed from the giant frame of Orson Welles, the suggestion that

Peppy could be the killer came almost as an anticlimax. 'There was something extremely familiar about your hat and coat. Aye, and even the false ginger moustache, was there not, Hargreaves?' I was forced to nod. Holmes continued, 'Miss Clovis, is it not true that you were at one time in your career other than an actress and model?' She shrugged, 'What of it, there was possibly a time when you were a well nourished and sharply dressed fellow, Cyril. Athough I rather doubt it!' Holmes bowed mockingly and turned to me, 'Hargreaves, toss that volume of the London telephone directory which is on the coffee table to Miss Clovis, if you will.' I picked up the directory that I confess I had purloined from a call box in order to be able to discover numbers at my leisure. This I was able to do provided the surname involved was between 'A' and 'D'. (Some crook had stolen the other books from the box already). I threw it to Peppy who fielded it with a surprising speed of reaction. Holmes said, 'Miss Clovis, would you oblige us with a demonstration of your amazing strength and tear that telephone book into halves?'

There was a silence that you could have cut with a knife. All eyes fell upon Peppy Clovis. At first she hesitated looking somewhat uncertain, then she seemed to cast all doubt aside and bracing the directory against her knee she managed to rip it into two, all but equal halves. She did it moreover with style and then said, 'Cyril you have done your homework well. I was indeed a strong woman, theatrically, for a while and billed as the 'Mighty Atom'. I have lived a far from blameless life as you have no doubt discovered, but I certainly neither killed Lionel Craig, nor attempted to shoot Joe McCarthy. I would like to have killed them both but I didn't! In fact your theory concerning the hat, coat and false moustache falls where it rises on account of the fact that they are not mine. I did not bring them here tonight. When you were all doing your turns I felt that I had to do something, so I slipped out and borrowed a hat and coat from the peg in the hall. The false moustache I found in the overcoat pocket. You must admit that it was heaven sent and added greatly to my impersonation?' Orson laughed and said, 'Peppy, honey, I'll cast you as a transvestite in a movie any time!' She wagged a finger at him and said, 'Hey, Orson, you know me better than that!'

Inspector Reynolds started to open the folded paper but yet again Holmes bade him not to. This surprised Reynolds who said, 'Mr. Raymond, your demonstration has been interesting but has served only to hint at one or two murky reputations concerning the suspects without proving any guilt in the Craig murder. All that your interesting demonstration has done has been to clear every one who has been under the cloud of suspicion.'

Holmes smiled mysteriously and said, 'All the words concerning guilt, innocence or somewhere in between have been yours Inspector. There has been a crime, a murder, and the name of the killer is written upon that scrap of paper. The person named is in this room, however much of a surprise you may consider this. Has it occurred to you that the murderer may not be someone named upon that list sent by McCarthy to Craig?' Reynolds nodded and said, 'Oh, yes, certainly, but you have told me that the person you have named is in this room. Surely you are not suggesting that you killed Craig yourself?' Holmes chuckled and said, 'Hardly Inspector, I would be incapable of doing so. Even were I able to have done the deed, you would be unable to imprison me, or bring me to trial, for reasons that I cannot at this moment divulge.'

The party atmosphere was long gone and every eye sped from Holmes to Reynolds and back again, like a crowd watching a tennis game. Then as a silence fell, all of the eyes tended to concentrate upon the policeman, and when he spoke there was an unexpected drama in his words and amazed expression. 'Are you suggesting, Mr. Raymond, that I committed this crime? I would remind you to be careful with your accusation because you are dealing with someone who has served faithfully as a police officer for twenty-five years, rising from the humble rank of constable to my present position through sheer industry and devotion to duty. Add to this, if you will, my complete lack of motive, indeed, my total disinterest in the affairs of the talking picture industry!' He made an all but apoplectic movement of his head as if about to continue, but in a rather less restrained tone. Holmes waved a placating hand. 'Please calm yourself, my dear sir, as I make no such accusation. Come you have not yet read the name that is written upon that scrap of paper that you are holding. I suggest that you do so now without perhaps showing it to anyone else, or reading aloud the name that appears upon it.'

The Inspector, calmer now, very slowly and deliberately unfolded the small sheet from my note pad and his eyes were closed as he did so. Then slowly his eyes opened and took on an amazed glint as he took in what he read. He was silent for perhaps twenty seconds before, having taken a swift look around the room, enquired of Holmes, 'So this person is guilty of both crimes in your opinion?' Holmes nodded. 'You have, I assume, some sort of proof to offer?' Holmes nodded again, 'I have, and I was actually present at the attempted assassination. You may see this for yourself if you re-show the newsreel. I assume you have a copy of it at Scotland Yard as well as the machine necessary to show it, Inspector?' Reynolds nodded, 'I see . . . and what first made you suspicious regarding this person, who may, or may not, be guilty?' (There was doubt in his voice).

'Many things but I suppose the first real certainty became implanted in my mind when I was considering the matter of the threatening letter, supposed to have been sent to Craig by Garrison. I considered the possibility of it being a forgery, considering that Garrison's headed notepaper could have been copied by this new photographic copying system. The signature may have looked genuine but the colour of the ink was wrong, and then the pen with which it had been written was suspect. I have made a study of fountain pens, their nibs and the effect of them on paper . . . ' (He paused and I prayed that he would not complicate things for us by mentioning his monograph on the subject. After all Reynolds was a Holmesian buff).

Holmes continued, 'The person concerned claimed to be a member of a musical group meeting regularly at a hall in this area. I slipped into one of their meetings uninvited and discovered that the music club was a bluff to cover the activities of an extreme left wing political organisation. I watched him also taking part in a socialist inspired march past this very window. I discovered that he wrote with an Onoto fountain pen, the nib and the ink of which would match the forged signature. When I found out that he was going to America on music club business and heard about the McCarthy rally that was to occur, I took myself off to that event and was able to save the Senator from Wisconsin from an early death. I was the man in the faded red robe, mentioned by the press yet unseen by the cameras. Take a look at the pen with which Hudson signed Hargreaves' rent book this evening and you will find that it is an Onoto!'

Reynolds turned to face Hudson who

stood near the door and said, 'Hudson, you had better let me take a look at your fountain pen. Oh, and Mr. Hargreaves, please let me see your rent book.' In surly manner, Hudson handed the pen to the Inspector who examined the item. As this was done Hudson spoke, 'You've got it wrong, Mr. Raymond, as anyone could have been wearing a coat and hat like mine, and a false moustache.' Holmes said, 'And also hung them in a hall thousand miles away?' Reynolds said, 'Why did you not appear on the newsreel?' Holmes replied, 'I think that my dressing gown has some effect upon the camera, but rest assured I was there and any press reporter who was there, and there were many of them, will describe me.'

Hudson retorted, 'You have no proof that I had anything to do with Craig's death, and I deny shooting at McCarthy!' But the Inspector was really interested now, especially at Holmes' next remark and the reaction it provoked. Holmes said, 'You were careless when you did not even bother to wear gloves when you broke Craig's neck and even handled furnishing in his office. I suppose you did not worry about fingerprints because you have no sort of criminal record and were over confident enough to believe that nothing would lead the police to your door.'

At this point I had grave doubts that Reynolds might be in a position to accuse, let alone arrest, Hudson. However, the wretched man, being of the limited intellect usually displayed by political extremists, made a trap for himself and jumped into it. 'This is my house and you can't arrest me without a warrant,' he shouted, 'I want to speak to my solicitor before I say anything else. As for you Raymond, you are just making up a pack of lies and I'll give you the back of my hand!' He advanced towards Holmes, his right hand upraised as if to strike him, but Reynolds grabbed him firmly and said, 'Mr. Hudson, I arrest you on account of using threatening behaviour towards Mr. Cyril Raymond. Anything you say . . . '

The police inspector continued telling

225

Hudson his legal rights. At this Hudson quite lost control of himself, screaming hysterically and shouting, 'I'm glad I killed Craig. He was a parasite in the pay of Joe McCarthy who is a fascist worse than Hitler. I'm only sorry that old scarecrow here stopped me from shooting the blackguard!'

Holmes muttered to me, 'He has saved us from a great deal of hard work, Hargreaves. I have no idea if he left any fingerprints, but the chances are that he did or he would not have lost his temper.' Then suddenly Hudson broke Reynolds' grip and made for the door which he tore open and slammed into the face of the Inspector who was trying to recapture him. I heard his frantic footfalls upon the stairs and then a piercing scream as the luckless man returned to the room. All attention was, of course, on the dramatic happenings near the door and when Holmes reappeared I realised that I had not noticed his going. It was obvious to me now that he had conveyed himself to the front door of the building and had not been too diplomatic in his manner of appearing in Hudson's path. This time the Inspector produced a set of handcuffs with which to restrain the prisoner.

Half an hour later we who remained of the party were still indulging ourselves in stiff nightcaps and trying to recover our nerves and vocal abilities to the point of discussion and even debate. Peppy, a little unsteady from a series of large gins said, 'Cyril darling, you are a wonder! You know, if you were a little bit younger you'd be perfect for playing Sherlock Holmes.' Holmes said, 'A medical man who was my only friend for many years once remarked that the London stage had been deprived of a considerable actor when I (he hesitated) took to other than theatrical pursuits.' Wayne Johnson said, 'Cyril old man, I dare not say what ran through my mind concerning your activities tonight. You are a gentleman and, more than that, it's my impression that you are an illusionist to rival Blackstone as well.' I tried to steer the conversation just a little right of centre, or may be that is an unfortunate phrase given the circumstances. Let's just say that I changed the subject. I said, 'You know, folks, this is one heck of an interesting little old country. I left Hollywood to get away from McCarthy, only to get involved in the most incredible situation in which he was one of the players. I've only been here a few months, but I've become that fat fish in a small pond that you mentioned, Orson!' Welles chuckled hugely and said, 'O.K., Greg, get your typewriter out. Am I too fat to be believable as Hudson?'

The following day as I was starting to clear up the sitting room, we had a visit from Inspector Reynolds. He told us that Hudson had made a full confession that made a perfect match of his fingerprints to those at the crime scene almost needless. He told me that I would be required as a witness. He turned to tell Holmes that he would also be needed, but the 'Ghost of Baker Street' had managed to do his disappearing act again. I tried to infer that Cyril had probably nipped out to the corner shop while we were talking. Reynolds looked at me keenly, 'Do you think he will willingly give evidence? If he doesn't, I have powers to force him.' I said, 'Oh, but that will not be possible, as no one can force Mr. Raymond to do anything.' He asked, 'What is it with him? Diplomatic immunity?' I said, 'No, supernormal powers!'

It transpired that Holmes completely failed to make himself available during the trial and for a few days thereafter. It made no difference, because Hudson presented no defence.

Epilogue

This really should have been the end of my story but this is not quite the case. You see, with the enforced removal of Hudson from his role as my landlord, I was placed in a position of uncertainty as to the future of my residence in Hudson House. I followed the trial avidly in what we colonials usually call the 'tabloids', and felt the smallest twinge of guilt when I read that the judge had donned the black cap. I was also relieved when this sentence was not carried out. After all, Hudson had claimed that my own involvement with Craig had been the 'camel's back breaker' that had spurred him on to violent action? The hanging was not carried out mainly through the sheer weight of public opinion, demonstrations and petitioning by the members of the International Music Guild saving Hudson from the long drop. Instead he would serve a life sentence which Holmes assured me would be reviewed and shortened later.

Quite soon thereafter, of course, the British Government discontinued capital punishment, save for in very exceptional circumstances and much of the thrill went out of contemporarily placed detective fiction. It is less of a strong climax if you can't hang the murderer, however barbaric that process might be. Writers, myself included, tended to backtrack and give a period setting.

I never quite got to grips with Holmes' opinions on the subject and he gave no hint as I read the paragraph concerning the last minute reprieve aloud. He had made himself scarce during the period of the trial for diplomatic reasons, but had returned in the last few days to take up a fairly regular residence in my flat. I call it mine for the sake of clarity, but of course, for a short period of time it would become nobody's property. There were plans afoot for its sale by auction to help pay for the defence. I finished reading the paragraph aloud and had turned to the property for sale columns. I knew that I had to find other accommodation eventually.

My eyes lit upon the unmistakable announcement . . . 'Desirable Victorian residence in Baker Street'. There followed a list of amenities and rooms, followed by the phrase, 'must be sold by auction for legal reasons'. I noted down the date, time and location of the sale and discussed the matter with Holmes. He began, 'Hargreaves, my dear fellow . . . ' (I knew enough about his character to be able to distinguish between his use of 'My dear Hargreaves' and 'Hargreaves, my dear fellow'. The former was purely polite, while the latter meant that he had some favour to ask). 'Could you not yourself make a bid for the property? After all, you are in funds through your television activities and I imagine it could be secured for a fraction of its true value.' I asked, 'Whatever makes you think that, for is it not indeed as stated 'a highly desirable Victorian residence'? Moreover I believe that sooner or later some shrewd operator will cotton on to the significance of the name 'Hudson House'. Some fan of your 'Boswell' Watson's work will figure out that it was once popularly known in 'fiction' as . . . ' He grunted, 'Oh, I don't know. There will be a viewing prior to the auction but the property might not appeal to those who view it.' I was surprised at this, 'Why ever not, for is it not a fine house in a good area of London? I don't think, even given my recent good fortune, that I could be in a position to buy it though.' He smiled enigmatically and said, 'We shall see, but I suggest that you attend the sale in any case.' This I could scarcely refuse to do.

Over the next weeks there followed a passing parade of viewers. Though not of the television variety, but those given permission to seek admission by the property agents of the law firm, Wilson, Montmorency, Clavering, Jones and Clavering (or something of the kind). These people would enter with a suppressed air of excitement, rather as if they knew something that I did not, but this would gradually change to one of apprehension. Indeed, this rather did puzzle me for quite a while until I caught Holmes 'at it'!

Usually he would not be at home when they called, or if he was he certainly made himself scarce. Then, unbeknown to me, he would make personal appearances on the stairs, or in any room into which I had not accompanied them. For example, there was a charming middle aged couple who arrived full of suppressed excitement and enthusiasm. He clutching a *Guide to Historic London* and she, to my concern, a leather bound volume of *The Exploits of Sherlock Holmes*. They fingered the oak doors and marble fireplaces with interest, almost affection, but whilst I was showing Mr. Harvey the living room, his wife dallied in the master bedroom. Suddenly an audible gasp, not quite a stifled scream, was heard from that direction. Mrs. Harvey emerged, obviously shaken, but saying nothing. Her interest in the property had ceased and, therefore, that of her husband.

After their polite but hasty departure, Holmes suddenly appeared in the bay window. I had put two and two together and asked, 'Holmes, did you deliberately appear suddenly in the bedroom to scare that poor woman?' He shrugged his bony shoulders. 'There was something in there that I wished to look at. I did not realise that you had visitors.' I asked, 'What was it you wanted to look at?' He shrugged again, 'I forget now. It was unimportant anyway.' I remonstrated, 'Holmes, you never forget anything. Did you also appear to Mr. and Mrs. Smithers, Mr. Boothroyd and Miss Hobley?' He shrugged yet again, defiantly, guiltily this time. 'I may have. I don't know why you are concerned about it. None of them screamed or fainted, did they?' I said warmly, 'Holmes, you really must stop these tactics that are not far short of sharp practice. You are trying to force down the value of the house by playing ghost! It is, to use one of your own favourite expressions, unworthy of you.' He smiled and spoke casually, 'My dear fellow, I don't know what you mean, but even though you have much to gain from them, I promise not to employ these tactics any more.' I laughed despite my finer feelings, 'It hardly makes much difference now, for the sale is tomorrow morning and it is already seven in the evening!'

The next day dawned bright. I had slept but little, I think on account of a second-hand guilty conscience. I decided to attend the sale as promised. The solicitor's agents had premises just off the Marylebone Road. The room where the auction was to be held was a large one with seating for perhaps a hundred people, but a quarter of an hour before the appointed time, I was almost alone in my seat in the back row. Nearer to the auctioneer there sat perhaps half a dozen people. These obviously legal types, with their bowler hats and briefcases, sat beside the auctioneer and conversed in a very morose manner. Eleven o'clock came and went, and by eleven fifteen they could scarce put off the evil moment any longer.

The auctioneer rose, lifted his little hammer and spoke in a dry tone that matched his acidic appearance. 'Ladies and gentlemen, good morning. We are here to dispose of, by auction, a most desirable property of Victorian origin in Baker Street, the details of which you will all be aware. You have each been given a specification and most of you will be familiar with the property through personal inspection. I am sorry to see so few of you here, but this means that some lucky buyer is going to get a real bargain!'

I glanced at these 'lucky buyers' and I have to admit that I could not spot anyone who seemed to present that persona. There was a hobo, or a 'gentleman of the road' as the British would call him, a woman with shopping and two children, doubtless taking advantage of an opportunity to rest her feet, and one other person, only to be described as a nondescript. Oh yes, and just as the auctioneer began to speak, one of the viewers whom I had met before walked in rather sheepishly, and sat near the front. The man who had the unenviable task of trying to sell Hudson House under such circumstances, droned on concerning its historic fixtures, spacious nature and excellent position. I assumed that he would need to withdraw the property from sale if he did not get a bid to match the very lowest price, or reserve, that he was permitted to accept. I do believe I nodded off for a few moments, because the next thing I remember was the auctioneer pointing accusingly at me and demanding, 'Your name, sir?' I muttered, Hargreaves, Greg Hargreaves! He wrote upon a sheet of paper and then to my horror I heard him say, as if in a dream (which I was still convinced that it was) 'Congratulations, Mr. Hargreaves, you have got yourself a bargain. Mr. Featherstone has accepted that we sell to you at two thousand guineas, which is well below the reserve price! If you would like to come down here, I have the contract for you to sign.'

I will not say that it was a nightmare, because when I considered it, I realised I could afford to pay the give away price of two thousand guineas. When I worked out what it was in 'real money' this seemed to make it sound even more like a bargain, but how had I managed to make a bid without recollection. Suddenly Sherlock Holmes spoke from behind me. I turned round and he explained the mystery. 'You were asleep, Hargreaves, and I knew that the opportunity could not be missed. I made a bid and pointed straight at you when the auctioneer looked up. Ventriloquism is not one of my talents but it was scarcely needed in this instance!'

Still, as if in a dream, I signed the various papers involved and gave the two gentlemen my cheque for two thousand guineas. It had all happened so quickly, but I could not be other than quietly pleased to be the new owner of Hudson House. After all, I had all but decided to remain in Britain as a resident. In fact I had even considered applying for British Nationality. Ownership of property would hardly harm such plans. There was also Holmes to be considered. It would be unfair for me not to at least try to provide him with a comfortable 'haunt' in which to rest his sparse old frame and hang his faded red robe.

At first I was happy simply to reside and work in comfort at Hudson House, but as time went by a rather interesting and lucrative plan entered my mind. I think this was suggested by the occasional visit which I would receive from

239

American tourists, who after getting over having the door opened by a fellow American, would enquire, 'Is this 221B Baker Street, residence of Mr. Sherlock Holmes?' I developed a stock reply just to be rid of them, 'There never was a 221B, and many houses have been said to be the one where Holmes resided.' Disappointed they would depart. Then, one day when examining my bank balance, I realised that I needed a second source of income to ensure my permanent residence in my new home. I decided to admit my tourist visitors and make a small charge for my time in showing them at least the flat that Holmes and Watson had once inhabited. In order to make this work, I decided I would need to decorate the sitting room in the exact style that my visitors would expect. I did what I could, with the portrait of Queen Victoria, a shelf of albums and portfolios, and a bench with microscope and test tubes. With a hammer and a blunt instrument, I made a fair representation of 'V.R.' in bullet holes in the wall, and my *pièce de résistance* was a bust of Holmes that I managed to get the girl sculptress, to whom I had rented the attic, to make for me. At night I lit the rooms so that its silhouette would stand out dramatically against the blind, and hence highly visible down in Baker Street.

Of course, at first Holmes thought that all these arrangements were for his benefit, especially when I spread pipes and tobacco about the place. When I explained my plan, he was surprisingly calm about it. Following early grouchiness he was very helpful with suggestions. He said, 'There never was a number 221B, as you have so rightly told your visitors, but Hudson House alone is not enough to pull in enough people to make your enterprise worth the effort. You cannot put that number on the door, but there is nothing to stop you re-naming the house. Provided you keep the existing street number, no one can stop you calling the house 'Two, Two One Bee' and that will be enough to give the clue to tourists of a Holmesian leaning!'

My first open day was not an

unqualified success, despite the modest entrance fee and the sculptress in a Victorian maid's costume taking the money on the stairs and selling copies of *Sherlock Holmes*, a satirical pamphlet of which I was quite proud. In fact, the only instance when there were more than two visitors at a time, there was a sudden exit by all four of them, making for Baker Street quite suddenly.

But on the second day, and from that time on, I have been quite bowled over by the interest shown. This has not been through advertising, but rather from simple word of mouth publicity. People start to turn up at ten in the morning, anxious to pay their entrance fees and buy their satirical pamphlets from my wife-to-be. And sometimes when visitors leave all too quickly, I turn to Margaret and say, 'It's Holmes, he's at it again!'

Books by Val Andrews
in the Linford Mystery Library:

SHERLOCK HOLMES AND THE
HOUDINI BIRTHRIGHT

SHERLOCK HOLMES AND THE
MAN WHO LOST HIMSELF

SHERLOCK HOLMES AND THE
EGYPTIAN HALL ADVENTURE

SHERLOCK HOLMES AND THE
YULE-TIDE MYSTERY

SHERLOCK HOLMES AND THE
GREYFRIARS SCHOOL MYSTERY

SHERLOCK HOLMES AND THE
SANDRINGHAM HOUSE MYSTERY

SHERLOCK HOLMES AND THE
THEATRE OF DEATH

SHERLOCK HOLMES ON THE
WESTERN FRONT

SHERLOCK HOLMES AND THE
TOMB OF TERROR

SHERLOCK HOLMES AT
THE VARIETIES

SHERLOCK HOLMES AND THE
CIRCUS OF FEAR

SHERLOCK HOLMES AND THE
BAKER STREET DOZEN

SHERLOCK HOLMES AND THE
SECRET SEVEN

SHERLOCK HOLMES AND THE
LONG ACRE VAMPIRE

SHERLOCK HOLMES AND THE
HOLBORN EMPORIUM

SHERLOCK HOLMES AND THE
HAMMERFORD WILL

THE TORMENT OF
SHERLOCK HOLMES

We do hope that you have enjoyed reading this large print book.

Did you know that all of our titles are available for purchase?

We publish a wide range of high quality large print books including:
Romances, Mysteries, Classics
General Fiction
Non Fiction and Westerns

Special interest titles available in large print are:
The Little Oxford Dictionary
Music Book, Song Book
Hymn Book, Service Book

Also available from us courtesy of Oxford University Press:
Young Readers' Dictionary
(large print edition)
Young Readers' Thesaurus
(large print edition)

For further information or a free brochure, please contact us at:
Ulverscroft Large Print Books Ltd.,
The Green, Bradgate Road, Anstey,
Leicester, LE7 7FU, England.
Tel: (00 44) **0116 236 4325**
Fax: (00 44) **0116 234 0205**

Other titles in the
Linford Mystery Library:

SHERLOCK HOLMES AND THE DISAPPEARING PRINCE

Edmund Hastie

The Crown Prince of Japan disappears without trace from his Oxbridge college rooms. Relatives of an heiress meet, one by one, with suspicious and grisly deaths. The thief of confidential battleship plans must be identified and located before the documents are leaked to the German military. And what nefarious activity links a cabman charging extortionate fares with a musically-minded butler? Narrated with wry affection by the long-suffering Dr Watson, each problem in this collection of four short stories showcases Holmes' well-honed skills of ingenious analysis and consequential deduction to perfection . . .